I0629694

Time in the Inside

By

Levern Fitzpatrick

This book is a work of fiction but is based on facts. This book has no strong language and should be reviewed by children of all ages. This book has been rated (PG). Parental discretion is not advised.

First printing, August 2009

Copyright @ 2009 by Levern E. Fitzpatrick, Sr.

All rights reserved

ISBN: 978-1-61584-922-2

Without limiting the rights under copyright reserved above, no part of this publication may be reproduced, stored in or introduced into a retrieval system, or transmitted, in any form, or by any means (electronic, mechanical, photocopying, recording, or otherwise), without the prior written permission of both the copyright owner and the above publisher of this book.

i

Dedication

This book is dedicated to my son Levern, Jr., to my daughter Anaya Lynn, to my mother, to my sister Rashanda, to my brothers Christopher, Sr., Michael, and Gregory, Jr. I can't forget my God-Mother Tina B., who has stuck by me for years and believed wholeheartedly that I could do and get done anything I desired. And to my brotha, business partner, and friend, Jefe (Chris), for helping me get to the next level in my everyday struggles. And to my big homey, Hakim (Dekie Davis), who was the first to review Time in the Inside and encouraged me to pursue my dreams and goals no matter what while sitting next to me in an 8x10 cell serving time at Trenton State Prison in 2000.

I also want to give a very special thanks to Pearl for doing her thing on this wonderful project. God bless sistah!

Table of Contents

Part 1

Chapter 1

The Crib

It was October 3, 1996; *Channel Six* news predicted the temperature to rise above seventy-five degrees that afternoon. At the wake hours of that fall morning, the temperature read fifty-five degrees on the thermostat center in Pleasantville on Main Street. At the South end of P'ville, in a medium- sized nicely furnished apartment, a seventeen year-old young man laid comfortably asleep on a queen size bed in one of three rooms. He was sprawled between grass- green satin sheets that matched the two night stands on each side of the spacious bed. At the foot of the bed, leaning against the wall was a dark green, six-drawer dresser with a half body length mirror on top. The position of the dresser made the full length, sliding glass closet door appear to be an immaculate bedroom set. In the corner next to the dresser sat a three-foot rack with a J V C stereo system on top. Caddy-cornered beside the two night tables sat two fifteen-inch Kenwood speakers, each connected to the stereo system that kicked a low, jazzy, surround-sound. Simultaneously, the youngster's pager and alarm clock beeped and buzzed, disturbing his rest.

"Dam it, man!" the youngster exclaimed from beneath the sheets.

He rolled over upset and reached on the night stand to shut the head throbbing noise of the alarm off. Sweat beaded on his forehead and slobber drooled down the corner of his mouth, which he wiped away with the back of his hand.

"Shit," he moaned angrily and discontinued the beeping of his pager.

Slowly, he rolled back over onto his stomach and deeply sighed at the unpleasantness of being awakened.

"Aww, man, damn, what the fuck man," he cursed out silently, after three thunderous knocks crackled through his bedroom door with an aggressive tone that loudly followed.

"Jerald!" the woman's voice hollered.

"Yeah, mom," the youngster mumbled back bitterly, reluctant to move.

"You know I don't like talkin' through no dag on door!" she barked intensely, in a very annoyed kind of way.

"I ain't dressed yet!" he aimlessly replied with a scratchy voice and grabbed one of the two fluffy pillows at the head of the bed, propped against the wall, to cover his ears.

His mother sucked her teeth and tried not to become angrier before turning away from his bedroom door. She thought about it and spoke to him calmly, knowing that would be the way to get him out of bed.

"There's some scrambled eggs, grits, and sausages on the stove. I'm about to get Crystal dressed, put her on the bus, and go to work myself."

Those words drew Jerald's attention. He jolted his head up, tossed his pillow in the air, and smiled. He cleared his throat and said,

"Aw'ight."

"Don't aw'ight me boy! Get your butt up and do somethin' with yo'self instead of drivin' that damn car around all day with no license!" she snapped, then walked away towards the bathroom. She stopped before entering and waited to hear a sarcastic remark.

"You hear me Jerald?" she asked meaningfully.

He grudgingly sat up on the edge of the bed. His pager began to vibrate again and the volume of his mother's words irritated him. He forced himself to feel awake, hoping that she would leave immediately.

"Yeah, yeah, I hear you," he replied, waving her off and rubbing the sleep from his eyes.

"Man, shhhhiiiiit," he grimaced sourly and yawned as he stretched for the pager.

"Damit, man," he said feeling tired from his long night of drinking Hennessy, smoking weed, and hustling.

"What's today?" he asked himself out loud, smelling the liquor seeping out of his pores.

"Oh, shit!" he yelled, suddenly remembering something. "Friday, damn!"

Jerald quickly stood up, causing blood to rush to his temples.

"Gotdamit," the youngster stated sharply, feeling his skull ready to burst.

He tossed the pager onto his bed, wrapped the top sheet partly around his waist as the rest fell loosely to the floor; then he opened the bedroom door.

"Mom," he called out childishly, trying to get his mother to deter her anger by the tone of his voice.

"Yeah," she responded from the bathroom while she was in the middle of helping her daughter dry off.

"Is Verna comin' home this weekend?" he asked.

She didn't answer right away; instead, she told her seven- year-old daughter to go to her room and start getting dressed.

"Good mornin' Jerald," the little, red-boned girl spoke in a tiny voice while darting out of the bathroom with a bright smile across her face, blanketed in a peach colored towel.

"Goodmornin' ya'self Red." Jerald smiled at the sight of his baby sister's pretty face.

The little girl was Carmel complexioned and light enough that you could see a hand print on her arm if it was squeezed hard enough. She had long brown, reddish hair like her mother's father hair color and hazel eyes like her dad. She possessed a combination of looks between both her parents, so the nick-name "Red" certainly described her well.

Their mother stepped out into the hall a second behind the girl and gave Jerald a quizzical stare, beading her eyes like a vulture hawking its prey.

"I don't know. Why?" she replied sharply to Jerald's question.

"Nothin', I just needed her to do somethin' for me, that's all."

His mother frowned before turning away to head for Crystal's room. She pivoted at the door and spat an abrupt remark.

"It betta not be for no illegal somethin'!"

6

"C'mon mom," Jerald whined.

"Don't c'mon mom me," she said and paused a second. "I'm not stupid Jerald; I mean it, it betta not be!"

She then disappeared into the room and attended to her daughter, leaving Jerald standing dumbfounded. Jerald shook his head and shut his bedroom door halfway. He took the sheet from around his waist, tossed it onto the bed, and grabbed a pair of thick, gray, Nike sweat- pants that was on the floor in front of the closet door. Before he put them on, he admired his bare physique in the full length mirror. Suddenly he became aware of what he was doing, which made him feel a little uncomfortable; he felt as if someone had been watching, so he pulled on his sweatpants quickly. He walked casually out of the bedroom, scratching his upper body and leaving ash marks of dryness all over. He stopped at his sister's bedroom door and peeped in slowly, watching his mother and little sister. His mother instantly noticed his presence.

"Why are you standin' there like that?" she asked, disturbed.

"I don't know," Jerald shrugged and leaned against the door panel. His mother's attention turned back to Crystal; she watched how the seven-year-old girl tied her sneakers with perfection.

"Boy, you haven't been smokin' that stuff again have you?" she asked assumingly.

Crystal shot him a wide-eyed look after stringing the second shoe.

"Nah, you buggin'," he smirked, trying to show his little sister that the question didn't bother him.

"You betta not be!" she said sharply. "I told you about messin' with that stuff." She eyed him coldly.

Jerald tried to sympathize with the aggression in her tone. But what could he have said to a mother that wasn't about to put up with or hear no drama. So he kept his mouth shut so no fuel would be added to the fire.

"What you need to do," she began firmly, speaking through her teeth, "is study for ya driver's license so you can look for a decent job, instead of sleepin' all damn day and runnin' all night. You also should be studyin' for your GED, since you wanted to quit school like you a man that pay bills and what not…Actin' like some damn pimp daddy or whatever you call ya self around here."

That angered him for sure, but he remained calm, ignoring his mother's truth.

"Is it the make-up mom? You got ya hair pulled back; is that's what's makin' you look different today?" he said coyly, to change the subject.

'What you talkin' about Jerald?" she replied.

"Yeah, mommy, you look pretty with make-up on and ya hair pulled back like that," Crystal complemented as well.

Their mother smiled and kissed her daughter's forehead with appreciation.

Jerald smiled harder, forcing the burning sensation he had stuck in throat down to his stomach.

"Thank you baby," she replied lovingly.

"Oh, I don't get a kiss? Jerald managed to say jokingly, knowing it wasn't likely to happen.

"Yeah, when you go and get'cha self together," she replied icily.

"Alright Crystal," she said. "We'll be set to go in a minute; mommy has to grab her briefcase and coat, so go grab your coat out of the closet."

"Which one should I wear mommy?" Crystal asked.

"Get your white and blue Polo jacket. It's supposed to be nice all day."

"Okay," Crystal replied and complied with her mother's request, opening her closet door to retrieve the Polo jacket.

"Come on Jerald, move out my way," his mother said and nudged a little.

"You need to go on child and do like I told you to do," she added as a matter of fact.

Jerald backed into the hallway, standing five-foot-eight, 162 pounds, having a slim physique and a six-pack stomach.

"Aw'ight ma, chill," he said playfully holding his hands up non-violently.

"I'll chill when you get ya self together," she remarked then added, "legally too. I'm not gonna keep tellin' ya ba'hind, and you better stop bringin' that expensive stuff in my house. My job pays me well enough for you not to have my privacy exposed by the authority." Then she entered her bedroom.

Jerald curled his lips up like Jay-Jay on *Good Times* and went into the kitchen for something to drink. Crystal went into her mother's room, ready to leave with her jacket in her hand.

"You ready mom?" she asked softly.

"In a minute honey; let me get these papers together neatly here, then we'll be set to roll."

Jerald walked quickly from the kitchen and passed his mother's room to avoid further confrontation. He went into his bedroom exhausted; he spread his arms out like a bird and collapsed face down onto the bed.

"Aww, yea," he sighed, closed his eyes, and drifted fast to sleep.

His mother and baby sister were finally ready to leave. Crystal slid her jacket on at the same time her mother rubbed her face with lotion.

"Alright baby, time to get outta here."

"Mom, you gonna pick me up today or let me catch the bus?" "I'll pick you up honey. Right now I want you

10

to go give your knuckle-headed brother a kiss good-bye and tell him to stay out of trouble."

"Okay," Crystal said happily and hurried to Jerald's room.

She stopped before entering, knowing how sensitive Jerald got when people walked in his room unannounced. Jerald lifted one eye open lazily to see his sister staring timidly through the crack of his door.

"What you doin girl?" he asked exhaustedly.

"Give me a kiss, so I can go to school," she said innocently.

A wide smile parted Jerald's lips as he noticed how independent his little sister had become.

"Come over here," he ordered, brotherly.

Crystal walked hesitantly to him with the tip of both thumb nails on the edge of her two top teeth. He quickly bear-hugged her and buried his face in her neck, while tickling her playfully and making animal sounds that caused her to laugh uncontrollably.

"Ah, I got you now," he said heartily.

"Stop it, stop it, stop it, you gettin' my clothes wrinkled!" she cried in laughter.

Jerald stopped after a minute so she could catch her breath, not worried about her pressed clothes. He thought to himself if his mother's going to yell at him let it be for something she actually sees. But then again, he'd rather not hear anymore than what he has. Jerald cuffed his sister's little oval shaped face with both his hands and kissed her lightly on the tip of her nose.

"Ewww," she said distastefully.

"Eww, what?" he replied, ready to play again.

"Ya breath stank," she said and pinched her nostrils with a smiling frown.

"Get outta here girl," he retorted animal-like. "I'll tickle you some more."

"No!" She jumped back giddily with her nostrils still clinched tight.

"You need to go brush ya teeth," she added.

"You betta get outta here." Jerald said

"I'm serious," she proclaimed, moving backwards towards the door in case she had to dash before he reached for her.

"Crystal, let's go baby; it's getting late," her mother called from the bedroom.

"Aw'right, here I come," Crystal shouted.

"I love you, Jerald," she said and leaped hastily into his arms to give him a big hug.

"I love you too, baby girl," he replied, hugging her and placing a kiss on her forehead this time. She pulled away to leave in a hurry, but made a sudden stop at the door. She spun around slowly and motioned with her pointer finger,

"I see you later, and stay outta trouble."

Jerald laughed heartily at his sister's sense of humor.

"You betta too, and be good in school."

"I will," she yelled back as she quickly walked to the living room door where her mother waited.

"Jerald, I'm gone. Make sure you lock the door before you leave," his mother said, and waited for his response.

"You hear me, Jerald?" she shouted loudly.

"All the time," he said sarcastically.

"Yeah, if you did you wouldn't do the things I tell you not to do!" she snapped and slammed the door.

"Bye, Jerrrr…," Crystal's voice faded in the wind.

He sucked his teeth at his mother's annoying remark.

"Whatever man," he sulked.

The pager vibrated a second later when he was about to doze off again.

"Goddamn, man, a nigga can't get no fuckin'sleep around here!" he complained irritably.

He snatched the pager from underneath the sheet.

"Who the fuck is this?" he looked at the pager angrily and annoyed. Jerald thought quickly, if he had his gun at hand he'd probably go looking for the "motherfucka" and shoot'em dead. But then again, the random and periodic page vibrations are part of being a full- time drug hustler.

He got up and stomped his way into the living room with the pager gripped tightly in his hand, ready to call the number. He waited a second until the other line finally rang a few times before someone answered.

"Hello," the male voice said, sounding like he had been smoking cigarettes for decades.

"Yo-who-dis?" Jerald said in one breath, sounding pissed.

"Yo, J.D., it's me man, Tommy," the voice identified.

"Oh, whad up T? I thought you was some crazy-ass chick, buggin'."

"Nah man, it's only me. Hey yo, I got that hundred dollas I owe you and two more!" Tommy exclaimed anxiously. "I get off work at two o'clock this evenin,', so can you meet me at the P.J's."

"Aw'ight, I'll be dere, no doubt," J.D. replied. "You betta be dere too nigga; don't have me waitin' all night or you gonna find ya self by ya self, follow me?" he added then hung up without waiting for Tommy's response.

Jerald's adrenaline began to pump so hard he could hear his heart thumping loud, like an African drumming in the Congo. That's what happens to hustlers when it's time to get that cash, he thought proudly.

14

He entered the room and grabbed the remote to his stereo system. He pushed the CD button and, instantly, the twelve-inch Kenwood speakers blared out "Get Money," by Biggie Smalls and the Junior Mafia. Jerald turned off his pager, lowered the volume on the stereo, peeled off his sweatpants, hopped back in bed, slid underneath the sheets, and fell fast asleep.

Chapter 2

The Dream

"Jerald, wake up! Wake up now boy! His mother screamed. A man stood next to her, whose face vaguely appeared. It seemed as if a thick cloud of fog was covering the man's features.

"Who's that wit you mom?" Jerald asked half sleep.

The man answered. "It's ya father boy; who else you want it to be? You heard ya motha, get yo ass up and do somethin' with ya life," he said, without moving his lips.

It was a strange moment for Jerald because he could hear those thundering words, but he couldn't understand why his father's mouth wasn't moving.

16

His father then turned and walked away, leaving Jerald and his mother to stare blankly. They both looked after him with tears streaming down their face. Jerald couldn't get himself out of bed; he felt heavy, bound in one position, as if bricks were holding him down.

"But it can't be," he thought. His father had been deceased for ten years. He had died in a motorcycle accident a week after Jerald turned six, and his older sister, Verna, was eleven. The three of them had been devastated by the death of Jack Jones, their father. Jerald was especially devastated because Jack was the only man in his life that did great things with him since he was born.

Jerald's mother had finished grieving the death of her husband and befriended Crystal's father a year and a couple months later. For Jerald and Verna, it had taken nearly several years to accept the fact that they would never see their father again. Even with Crystal's father came in their life, Jerald didn't allow Crystal's dad to replace his father's absence. Nevertheless, the possibility of that happening ended a few months after Crystal's birth; Trevor Davis, Crystal's father, bailed out of their lives, leaving Jerald's mother with three fatherless children in the projects of Atlantic City with not even a penny to wish on. Gloria Doley had no option at that time of their lives but to move to a smaller apartment, refusing to watch her children become victims of rape, murder, and violence. Gloria prayed that her situation didn't force her to be at her lowest point in life.

17

Jerald woke up frantically, drenched in sweat, while his heart raced violently. He then realized it was all a dream...

Chapter 3

The Time

One-thirty in the afternoon, Jerald finished dressing, feeling completely revived from being able to sleep most of the morning without the disturbance of his pager, alarm clock, and, not to mention, his mother's radical bangs on the bedroom door. He also couldn't ignore the voice of his father and the vague figure in his dream.

Jerald picked up the remote to the stereo and cranked up the volume a little to listen to his favorite song by Tupac, "I Get Around", before he left. He quickly glanced around the room, searching for his car keys as he fastened his Guess watch to his wrist. His watch had a black face, a glow-in- the-dark minute and second hand, all attached to a silver water-proof band. He immediately recollected where his keys were; they were underneath the mattress so his mother wouldn't find them to stop him from driving or coming in late at night. He placed the alarm in his front pocket while the few keys he had on a single silver ring dangled outside his pocket. He dabbed some Muslim oil called "Smiley Rose" onto his hands, and then rubbed it on his face and neck.

Jerald smiled widely as he scrutinized his fashionable appearance in the full length closet mirror. He then grabbed his pager and the two, hundred dollar bills lying on his neatly made queen- size bed. He stuffed the money in the front pocket, opposite the pocket where his keys were hanging. He clipped the pager to his leather belt that held his pants appropriately in place. He snatched the remote off the bed and did a few dance steps in the mirror before shutting the stereo off. Jerald pivoted a second to make certain there was nothing he was leaving behind.

He mumbled to himself, "Aw'ight nigga, it's on," then hurried out and closed his bedroom door behind, hoping he didn't run into his mother coming home for a lunch break. He continued his way out the apartment, remembering to lock the door on the way out. Jerald strutted down the narrow corridor of the complex to the stairway. He anxiously leaped two flights of steps at a time, making a quick exit to the ground floor. He cautiously approached the back exit door stutter steps, hoping he wouldn't run into anyone he recognized. The coast was clear, so he swiftly pushed the steel exit door open, only to find him self getting hit.

"Shit!" he exclaimed loudly, looking down at his Lug boots.

"Oh, sorry about that young man, I didn't expect anybody to be comin' out this way," an elderly man said, expressively sounding weary from pushing a shopping cart, which collided into Jerald when he opened the door.

"'That's aw'ight," Jerald stated politely, getting annoyed.

"Nice shoes you have on there," complimented the old man.

"Thanks," said Jerald in return, wishing he could smack the old man his mother knew very well.

"Well, you be careful now, sorry about that again," the old man said apologetically, making his way past Jerald to get to his apartment on the first floor as Jerald considerately held the door for him to go in without further collision.

"No problem," Jerald mumbled to the old man.

The old fellow cleared the door entrance, looking carefully not to run into anything else, and waved his hand, unconcerned, without looking back. Jerald let the door close.

"Damit!" he exclaimed angrily. "Old bastard needs to watch where the fuck he's goin'."

Jerald bent down to wipe the scuff mark off his left boot where the old man's cart accidentally ran into him.

"Fuck it," he said frivolously and continued to walk towards his parked 1993, cherry red, Cobra Mustang GT. Jerald's anger subsided quickly at the sight of his hot car, which was pulled beside a big, red good- will dumpster. He eagerly pulled out his car key to disarm the alarm from about five paces before he reached the car.

"My Cobra clutch," he said with a proud smile. Jerald opened the door and hopped in carelessly, started the car, pressed hard on the gas pedal several times with maximum pressure to hear the V8 engine roar with power. Since Jerald had little experience with cars; it was fortunate that he was able to find this particular mustang with an automatic shift, because a five-speed was something he definitely couldn't drive. He turned on the CD player and cranked up the stock Kenwood system. The six by nine speakers screamed, *"Brooklyn's Finest,"* by rap icon Jay-Z. Jerald closed his eyes, tilted his head back for a moment, allowing the adrenalin to subside, while his foot remained on the brake, his car resting in park mode. He rocked his upper body to the beat, feeling the encouraging words of Jay-Z's song, which also featured the rap legend Notorious B.I.G.

He took his foot off the brake and reached into the glove compartment; he pulled out a Philly cigar and quickly un-wrapped it. He threw the plastic out and split the blunt down the center. The temperature was growing hotter by the minute, yet it was still a beautifully calm

22

afternoon. Jerald snapped his fingers and tried to figure out where he placed his weed.

"Ok, Ok," he said with a sly grin, remembering where he hid it.

He reached under the driver seat and grabbed a black tape cassette case; in it laid three, large, light green marijuana buds. A sense of pride warmed Jerald's temple. He took one of the weed buds and crumbled the crispy leaf into the open center of the Philly cigar; then he steadily and delicately rolled it up. He looked around the parking-lot cautiously to make sure there wasn't anyone in sight. He licked the loose end of the blunt across its top, and then he twisted it so it would stick better. Jerald reached for a red lighter as he placed a green and red marijuana leaf on each side of the consol. He lit the blunt and took a long, polluted, drag to feel the sensational effect. He exhaled the smoke slowly as he opened up the sun- roof and slid the windows to let the smoke drift out.

Jerald put his right foot back on the brake pedal and pulled the gear-shifter into drive. He pulled out of the parking lot slowly, still puffing on the cigar as his eyes-lids shrieked smaller from the instant gratification of the high. He looked at his watch and noticed that it was almost time to meet Tommy.

"Damn," he said, lowly, "I gotta meet this nigga at the jetz, shit."

Jerald started to become a little paranoid, scanning the perimeter of parking lot sharply before entering old

Blackhorse Pike. He decided he wouldn't take that route, so he eased back into the parking lot and turned around. He could exit out the other end of the complex, he thought; there was a short- cut to get to the Projects in Atlantic City and he needed to meet up with Tommy and the other crack feigns before the other niggas got the money.

Chapter 4

The Stake-Out

Two under-cover cops on a surveillance stake-out prepared for the suspect to arrive. Mc- Greed, the rookie cop, was eyeing the area through a black and silver telescope that could probably extend about three feet. They were parked behind an abandoned Cavalier that had two flat tires, a clear plastic cover placed over the front window shield, and a coating with orange rusted spots that blended with the old, faded rust colored paint job.

"Right on time, pal," Mc Greed said out loud. "He's in plain view Detective," he added.

Detective Perkins sat on a milk crate behind Mc Greed and faced the opposite direction as he watched the suspect on the computer- looking monitor connected to the video camera; the camera pointed through a peep hole next to the telescope. Mc Greed handled the video camera while it recorded part of Pacific Avenue near the corner of Tennessee Avenue.

"This kid never fails," Perkins said and shook his head in disbelief.

"From what he's been raking in monthly, hell, I probably wouldn't stop either, especially working for myself at his age" Mc- Greed stated.

"Yeah," the Perkins agreed, "but there has to be a source this kid is gettin' his stuff from. I don't believe he has a mountain of drugs stashed in his house or car. This kid got a supplier somewhere close."

"Sure you're right, and the only way we'll find out is when you make the call for him to fall!" Mc Greed exclaimed impatiently.

"Patience Frank; maybe his supplier will slip up sooner or later and that way we can try to get two for one, you know," Perkins advised, but didn't believe it himself.

The two undercover agents sat in silence for a brief moment in deep thought. Mc Greed went back to watch the suspect from the telescope to the camera. Perkins sipped on a cup of lukewarm, dark roasted, 7-Eleven coffee and stared at the screen.

"Don't know," Mc Greed mumbled breaking the silence, "with that nice ride he just bought. His supplier, if he has one, might not have a good reason to visit him out here."

Perkins gave it some thought before he responded.

"Maybe," he continued, "this past month, watching this kid gives me the impression that his supplier could just be local." He paused; "shit, he hasn't been anywhere but to them damn projects."

Mc Greed quickly said, "Do you think?"

Perkins read Mc Greed's thoughts before he completed the sentence.

"Aww," Perkins sighed, "that's where his source could be located."

A thin smile crossed Mc Greed's lips as he shook his head up and down.

"Listen," said Perkins, "check in with dispatch to find out if a convicted drug felon named Walley Watson, a.k.a. "Winky," is around the neighborhood."

"Gotcha," Mc Greed said, and then moved quickly to the radio headquarters. Perkins sat quietly, eyes glued to the screen.

"We got you now J.D., Mr. Pusher." Mc Greed responded while hunched over in a cramped van,

"Nothing," he said, disappointed.

"Damit!" Perkins shouted angrily.

"We have to wait until we take him, and then we can see what we can get out of him; maybe he'll talk once we apply a little pressure. We just got to get closer to him so we can get enough evidence to really squeeze the vice; that way he'll be willing to spill his guts." Perkins advised

Mc Greed looked at Perkins and nodded in agreement.

"Yeah," Mc Greed said, then he added, "but didn't you take him down before?"

"Yes," Perkins answered, "and you see where he is now; the damn system don't seem like it's working in our best interest sometimes. I mean, we sit out here bustin' our asses to catch little pricks like this, them to only get a year on probation." Perkins stressed, and then continued.

"I should have built more evidence on him before, just like we're doin' now. Maybe his ass wouldn't have been back on the streets so damn fast, doin' the same shit."

"Right," Mc Greed replied, then kneeled on one knee to look back through the telescope.

"Honestly," Perkins said, feeling the need to share a truthful story, "I never wanted to get involved with these drug cases before," he paused, "I figured pushing the paper work would have been delightful enough to do every day and I could go home safely, unknown to anyone with a decent pay check to take home every week," he took a deep breath before continuing, "until my nephew got killed a few years back over some drug beef. It broke my sister down for months, so I promised myself that I would take every drug dealer down in my city if it was the last thing I did."

Perkins said nothing else for a few minutes after that. Mc Greed had listened attentively and knew that his intentions were totally opposite. Mc Greed passed on the opportunity to share why he wanted to see drug dealers off the streets. The truth probably wouldn't have gone over well with Perkins, especially because Mc Greed was a white cop and he was a black cop.

"It's Friday, supposedly a big money day for the dealers, so that should throw him off later on. Right now, let's just sit back, relax, and allow the video camera to do the work. Then we'll move in when it's time. Oh, and the answer to that question about takin' him down is I bought drugs from him by posing as a potential client a few times, but I wasn't the one that made the arrest. I had a couple, other under- cover officers take him. The kid never took it to trial, so all was ended quickly," Perkins mentioned as a matter of fact.

"I don't believe this fuckin' guy," Mc Greed said doubtfully.

"He just dropped outta school last year and been sellin' drugs for a couple years now. He's not interested in what's around him. His main objective is money, material, and attention. He's just like the average drug dealer with nothin' else on his mind, trust me, nothing at all." Perkins assured Mc Greed while his eyes stayed glued to the monitor.

Mc Greed exhaled slowly and took a seat on another crate next to Perkins. The detective smiled with certainty and patted Mc Greed on the shoulder.

"Relax Frank, there's no need to rush, he's a kid. He has no, no intuition, and no direction. I hate to keep classifying these kids but he's actually wandering without a sense of purpose like many other kids and even some adults. But we'll get'em, it's all about timing" Perkins said, knowingly.

Mc Greed rubbed his face tiredly, placed his elbows on his knees, and cuffed his knuckles under his chin for head support. He watched the screen as his blood boiled.

"Jeff," Mc Greed called Perkins by his first name.

Perkins responded sharply and looked out of the corner of his eyes at Mc Greed.

"Sorry 'bout that detective," Mc Greed said apologetically, not knowing what to expect.

"No, no, it's ok, as long as the team doesn't hear you call me that," Perkins said, not wanting to sound pissed about it.

"Thanks," 'Mc Greed replied with a smile, then continued, "I just wanted to ask you, how many drug raids have you been in?"

Perkins exhaled sullenly to the grotesque question before he answered.

"Too many," he replied reluctantly.

"Have you ever been in any shoot outs?" Mc Greed asked timidly, but curiously.

"Yeah"

"Any deaths?" Mc Greed went on.

Perkins dropped his head a minute and pondered the question.

"I'm afraid so," he said, and smoothly caressed his dark, thick, black mustache," then added, "I've been on the force for fifteen years Frank, and I really get sick of watching these young kids and adults destroy their lives over drugs, violence, and sex, you name it. It doesn't make any sense. I mean some of them are going to do what they feel is necessary to do, whether it's for survival or whatever. It's nerve racking to me though. Don't get me wrong; shit, half of them need to be behind bars for the crimes they committed, but others, like these children out here, really need another alternative than prison or death. I'm not trying to contradict what I said a few minutes ago about taking all the drug dealers down that I can, but for crying out loud, kids like this guy, Jerald, don't have a clue. They're babies and need to find out their potential in life. I, I, I can't go on. I'm not gonna preach about it no more; it's useless."

Mc Greed appeared to be listening, but he was in his own thoughts, then he swung around on the crate to take another look through the telescope.

"He's making another sell!" Mc Greed exclaimed quickly and took his mind off the possibility of becoming lenient.

"Ok," Perkins answered, "let the camera keep rollin'." He paused a second then asked Mc Greed,

"You got any family Frank?"

Mc Greed withdrew from looking out of the scope.

"No, I'm a bachelor," he said.

"You know, after I graduated out of the academy, I said the hell with a family, until I run into a compatible woman to my liking that can share the same unique qualities that I possess," Mc Greed stopped then asked Perkins another question.

"How about you detective, you have a family?"

"Nah, not me," Perkins replied with a smile.

"Sometimes I wish…I was married once though. It didn't work out that long; no kids came out of it."

"How long you've been an officer?" Perkins questioned.

"Come on detective, like you don't know."

"If I did, I wouldn't have asked."

"You're not jokin'?"

"Nope, I never looked in your file. I just seen somethin' about you and felt as though you would be the perfect officer to train with as an undercover," Perkins admitted.

"Thanks, that's a pleasure to hear," Mc Greed said with a little sense of pride.

"Well, I've been an officer for about three years now. I've been trying for detective for the longest. That's why I transferred here to Atlantic County. I didn't see any future in Frankford Township."

"I know what you mean; maybe that's what I seen in you."

"What's that?" Mc Greed asked curiously.

"Ambition, motivation, and a potential to be more than just an officer walkin' around handin' out unnecessary parkin' tickets and other minor citations," Perkins grinned.

"Thanks detective."

"Don't mention it. Just perform as you would have before you knew my personal observation of you, that's all."

"Will do," Mc Greed said gratefully and looked at the screen, then jumped on one knee to zoom the telescope in on the suspect.

"He's leaving detective."

"He'll be back, trust me; that's his corner," Perkins assured Mc Greed.

"We'll move out once he returns which will probably be an hour or so from now. Things won't be rollin' until a little later anyhow; there'll be more traffic for us to blend in."

"Gotcha," Mc Greed answered, encouraged.

Chapter 5

The Block

Back on the block of Pacific Ave., exactly one hour later as detective Perkins had predicted, Jerald, a.k.a. J.D., pulled out a knot of hundred dollar bills he had made so early in the day.

"Aye, yo, whad'up Pete?" He called out to a buddy he use to go to school with, who was also walking with another school kid.

"Ain't nothin' Jay, how you dog?" the five-foot-eleven, brown skin, young boy replied as he greeted J.D. with a hand dap.

"Just coolin', doin' me, you know," J.D. said and gave Pete a million dollar smile.

"Yeah, I feel you," Pete nodded.

"Ayo, is that ya whip over there on the street?" Pete asked and nodded his head in the direction of the car.

"What the stang?" J.D. replied boastfully.

"Yeah, that Jawn is tight dog, word," Pete expressed with admiration, staring at the shining car.

"Yeah, that's me; I just copped dat a few weeks ago," J.D. answered frivolously, realizing how the two boys were amazed.

"So how's school, dog?" J.D. asked, changing the subject.

"Its aw'ight, you know, I'm makin' it, me and my manz, Kevin here. We be pushin' each other to get through this thing, feel me."

"Yeah, I definitely feel that," .J.D. replied, unenthused.

"So, what, you just moved around here kid?" Jerald asked the baby face, high yellow, curly- headed kid standing next to Pete as he looked him up and down observantly.

"Nah," Kevin answered scarcely, with a thin smile, revealing pearly- white teeth.

"Nah, J.D.," Pete intervened, "Kevin lived around here all his life, and he's from the west side of the city. He's been in school; he's just came back to a public this year. He was in the Viking Academy School. Kev's low-key now, trynna stay outta trouble, you know," Pete finished, noticing the fear Kevin's eyes showed.

"Word, word, that's the way to be these days," J.D. stated assuredly.

"Check, we gonna spin off, you know, let you do you," Pete exclaimed quickly giving J.D. another hand dap.

"Aw'ight, dog, dig, any time y'all lookin' for an easy way out, look me up, follow me," J.D. said with persuasively as Pete and Kevin began to stride away.

"I'll holla," Pete yelled out over his shoulder.

"Yea, do dat," J.D. said and added sarcastically as he spat on the pavement, "punk ass niggas."

"Be easy yo," Kevin managed to shout back, feeling a sense of ease leaving J.D.

"Yeah, one," J. D. mumbled sinisterly, "Niggas lucky I don't got my heat."

He then turned his attention to a red Ford Escort that pulled over to the corner where he was standing with two people in it.

"Hey, whad'up?" J.D shouted out waving his arms in the air at the pulled over vehicle.

"Let me get two," the passenger requested in an eerie tone appearing frail in the face.

"You got the money for two?" J.D. asked aggressively to the dark skinned man before making the transaction with him.

"Yeah, yeah, yeah," the buyer replied hastily.

"Don't be playin' me yo. In fact, step out the fuckin'whip now. I don't trust you mothafuckas," J.D. ordered harshly.

"I'm not playin' Jay, man, I'm straight," the man pleaded nervously, realizing how ruthless the young drug dealer could be towards drug addicts.

"Aw'ight," J.D. warned, unconcerned if the dark complexioned man complied or not. J.D. whipped out a wallet sized, black leather pouch with several zippers. He unzipped the top and pulled out two tiny plastic Ziploc baggies with tiny, hard, tan, rock forms.

"Y'all a be back after y'all taste this fish scale, fo'real," he boasted, taking the money first from the crack feign before handing him the tiny baggies.

"Ok, ok," the drug user hurriedly replied with his hands cuffed together to make certain not to drop the two tiny baggies, as his eyes grew wider.

J.D. quickly tossed the two baggies into the junkie's hand after he made sure the money was correct. The driver of the vehicle pulled away in a hurry, screeching the car tires while the tail pipe blew out intoxicating exhaust fumes, polluting the city air.

"Damn!" J.D. exclaimed and fanned his hands to clear out the unbearable smell. He shook his head, disgruntled, and then he turned his direction towards the north end of the block, where he saw other children getting off the school bus. Standing across the street was a beautiful girl that he admired a lot. She was waiting for the buses to pass so she could walk across Pacific Ave. J.D. spotted her, looking pretty as ever, wearing a peach colored sun dress, a matching cotton- net sweater, and a pair of DKNY saddles. She was a radiant little lady; her long, jet black, curly hair, neatly placed out of her face, swayed as she walked.

"Damn, girl," J.D. said under his breath lustfully, watching the Carmel complexioned female walking in the opposite direction of him.

"Aye, yo," he called out, "yo, Shemika!"

He strained a little louder with a temper. "Oh, oh, it's like that, huh?" he said as he made a funny gesture with his hands to get her to smile while he approached her.

"You know I don't get down like that, so why are you callin' me?" she snapped with a twisted frown.

"Oh, but when I was broke wit' holy sneaks on goin to school, you act like you was all wit it then!"

"Then, is right," she barked sarcastically and stepped closer to him, "when you was in school doin' somethin' positive and productive with your life."

"What you talkin' about, I am doin' somethin' positive; I'm a hustla, I got money, a car, whatever you,

39

the ladies, lookin' for," he boasted stupidly pointing to his cherry red mustang. "My gear stays phat, so whad 'up?"

"I'll tell you for the last time," she said shaking her head and spelled out loudly, "No, get your E.D.U.C.A.T.I.O.N, that's what's up. You think this drug life is what it's all about, but you'll see the big picture one day which will be your reality check, not mine."

"Now you wanna hate," he said eyeing her lustfully as she walked away, lusting her sexy walk. Suddenly she stopped, turned around, and took a few steps back towards him, squinted her eyes, and tightened her lips. "I don't hate on any one negro, especially a loser. You just don't get the picture and I don't have time to stand here and enlighten you on what you should already know, when it's just only going to go through one ear right out the other," she concluded, snapped her finger, and continued walking.

"Whatavea hater," J.D. replied, feeling insulted, "you'll see; I'm a get mine." His words faded with a wave of the hand.

"You most certainly will," she agreed from a distance; "but what you need to do is get a job. See ya," she said out loud, leaving him dumbfounded.

"Yeah, peace, hater," he shouted, stung.

Shemika gave him the middle finger and continued down the block and around the corner. J.D. was pretty upset; he didn't expect to be dismissed by the one female he held deep feelings for. His first instinct was to run her down and go postal, but he sided against it quicker than he thought about doing it. Instead, he pulled out the black pouch and began counting the little baggies inside to take his focus off what had occurred and got back to business as usual.

Mc Greed and Perkins sat in the van. They paid very close attention to the harsh dismissal of Shemika's words, but, most importantly, her actions.

"That kid will never see the light at this rate," Perkins said, and shook his head with a pleased smile.

"Wow, that's what I call a shut down; she's a smart chick," Mc Greed said impressed.

"Yeah, she definitely is," Perkins added.

"You ready boss?" Mc Greed eagerly asked.

"Let's wait for about five more minutes, see what happens."

"Five minutes, detective we got this little drug dealing scum bag right now," Mc Greed said impatiently.

"One more transaction," Perkins replied calmly, "that way we'll have a much stronger case for the prosecution, especially after we make the buy ourselves."

"You're the boss," Mc Greed said silently.

"You're right," Perkins agreed clearly.

The two undercover cops watched the drug solicitation through each surveillance instrument for fifteen minutes longer.

"One more sell...we can't afford to see probation this time, no fuckin' way," Perkins said resentfully.

"I'm wit ya, hundred percent," Mc Greed said supportively.

"Damit, it takes no time for this fuckin' kid, but I told you, it's a money day and he's not paying attention to nothin' else but that," Perkins exclaimed irritably. "You remember your roll because we have no room for fuck ups, not right now?" he asked Mc Greed while they prepared for execution.

"Gotcha," Mc Greed said silently, causing Perkins to eye him hard for reassurance.

"Yes, sir," Mc Greed reiterated.

"You ready?" asked Perkins.

"Anytime you are, boss," Mc Greed exclaimed concealing his badge that was clipped to his belt underneath his kaki jacket.

The two officers hunched over to ease into the front driver and passenger seats. They both looked around behind the tinted windows, making sure no one was walking in their direction that could expose their identity.

"Clear on this side, detective, Mc Greed said.

"Let's move out," Perkins finally ordered.

Both undercover cops quickly left the van on the passenger side leaving the surveillance equipment to run so they would have a solid conviction. The two cops walked to the back of the van, opposite where the surveillance camera was pointing.

"Let's take the corner and come around," Perkins suggested.

"You don't think he'll make you, do you detective?" asked

Mc Greed.

"Nah, like I said, he didn't dispute the last charges, and I didn't bust him," Perkins explained again, as they made their way around the block, blending in with the other pedestrians getting off work and loitering in front of the stores.

The two men made it around the block in minutes. J.D. immediately spotted them approaching his way. Perkins was six-foot, slender, had broad shoulders, a light brown complexion, and wore a nappy afro. He sported a thin burgundy jacket, Levi Jean's that were worn at the knees and buttock's area, and white and gray New Balance sneakers run down in the front , giving him the appearance of a typical drug user look. J. D's first impulse was to jet, figuring the two men were cops, but he stood instead, staring at the light brown man approaching, trying to recollect if he knew him. Perkins and Mc- Greed closed in; J.D. shook his head and smiled as he recognized Perkins was an old costumer. He took a couple steps towards the two men.

"Whad'up money?" he said firmly.

"Hey J.D., what's up man?" Perkins replied, showing pearly white teeth.

"Long time, playa," J.D. said remembering Perkins' face vividly.

"Yeah, it has been." Perkins smiled back confidently.

"What you lookin' for, that fish scale today?" J.D. asked, staring Mc Greed up and down suspiciously.

"What you got for mc Jay, it's been awhile," Perkins said noticing him eyeing Mc Greed curiously.

"Hold up... this catz a cop!" J.D. exclaimed and stepped back in position to run.

"Come on Jay, what are you talkin' about man; he ain't no damn cop," Perkins managed to say in an offensive tone, realizing he shouldn't have taken Mc Greed along or betray his partner's identity.

"Dude, get serious," Mc Greed responded resembling a five-foot- eleven surfer with a thin physique, dirty blond hair, and an unshaved face, wearing his famous blue kaki jacket, faded black jeans and a old pair of warn down deck-side shoes.

"I bought from around here before dude," Mc Greed spoke up.

"So what that mean" J.D. replied temperedly, still trying to decide if he should run or not.

"I don't mess around yo, special things is in special places, and this ain't no special place, dude!" he emphasized, "not for no unknown jokers like you anyway."

"Listen, Jay man, you dealt with me before," Perkins reaffirmed.

"And what the fuck that mean?" he said to Perkins really pissed off.

"And you should know I wouldn't bring no cop to you!" Perkins exclaimed quickly.

"Hey, dude, forget all the special places we could be, if you don't like me for some unknown reason dude, then fine, I'll split."

"Wait, wait, wait a minute now wait a goddamn minute," Perkins said and stopped Mc Greed from walking away.

"What dude?" Mc Greed said, pretending to be aggravated and offended.

Perkins stepped closer to J.D. and cautiously placed one hand on J. D.'s shoulder, hoping it wasn't a risky move.

"Listen, Jay man, this really offends me, he's not what you think. I wouldn't dare do that to a brotha on the block, better yet period, you know what I'm sayin'," Perkins said lightly.

J.D. gave Perkins an evil look, but imagined dollars signs, which eventually subdued his anger.

"So come alone next time," J.D. replied and jerked his shoulder away from Perkins' friendly touch.

"I don't have time for this extra comp'ny, shit, you got me. out here, mothafuckas doin' all kinds of crazy shit. I don't know what jackasses are up to today; niggas be wildin' and this mothafucka looks like a damn cop," J.D. stressed seriously.

Perkins hesitated for a second appearing to be ambiguous about the situation.

"Look," Perkins began, "he'll roll if it'll make you feel more secure, alright?" Perkins gave Mc Greed the eye signal, undetected. "Frank, you go ahead and roll. I'll catch up with you in a minute or so."

"No sweat, dude," Mc Greed replied.

Mc Greed set off down the block to the corner of Pacific and Tennessee Ave. J.D. smiled inside, concealing his victory.

"Everything straight now, Jay?" Perkins asked quickly as if he was preparing to get the deal over with.

"Next time, I'll bounce without the trouble," J. D. spluttered arrogantly, "I don't like fuckin' wit catz I never dealt with before."

"You got that, Jay." Perkins agreed.

"So what you want anyway," J. D. asked anxiously, as he dug into his pocket for the little leather pouch.

"I need the usual specials man," Perkins answered fervently.

"I don't remember the usual," J. D. replied and looked at Perkins conspicuously.

Perkins noticed the stare and disregarded it.

"Give me five specials," Perkins reached into his own pocket and pulls out a wad of money neatly rolled in a rubber band.

He and J.D. were hesitant for a minute; then J.D. dug five of the tiny pebbles out of the zippered pouch and handed them to Perkins.

"Is that all you want?" J.D. asked, expecting Perkins to purchase more because of the knot of money he displayed nonchalantly.

"Yeah, I guess so," Perkins replied.

"You sure, yo?" J.D asked influentially while he looked down into the black pouch.

"For now," Perkins said with a sinister grin.

Mc Greed had his head peeped around the building watching the entire transaction. He noticed Perkins' grin; that was his cue; it was time to move in quickly.

"I know you'll be back after you try this shit, word," J. D. said not paying any attention to Mc Greed approaching from behind him.

"Not for you, of course!" Perkins exclaimed sharply.

"What you…? J.D. began to say, but stopped in mid-sentence to see his eyes staring down the barrel of Perkins' nine millimeter pistol, pointing in his face at close range.

"Oh, shit!" J.D. shouted surprised and unable to move or think.

"Freeze, you little shit head! Police! Don't fuckin' move!" Mc Greed and Perkins said simultaneously.

"Get down now! Now!" Mc Greed shouted hastily from the back of J.D. with his gun nearly touching against J.D.'s skull.

"Ok, ok," J.D. uttered softly, complying slowly with Mc Greed's order.

"You're under arrest for the distribution of narcotics to an undercover police officer," Perkins began to say placing his gun back into his shoulder holster while Mc Greed aggressively shoved J.D into the concrete with his foot as he gripped his gun tightly.

"You have, the right to remain silent, you have the rights to an attorney, and anything you say can and will be held against you in the court of law," Perkins advised.

"Do you understand the rights I just read to you Mr. Jerald Doley?"

"Awww, man, you a fuckin' cop, damn, damn," J.D. cried, not comprehending the situation.

"I'm surely not the fairy-tale brotha," Perkins remarked sarcastically.

"I had a fuckin' gut feelin; I shouldn't of did this shit," J.D. mumbled under his breath, in tears, with his hands straight out to the side.

"What's that, special boy?" Mc Greed asked victoriously with a bright smile and grabbed J. D's wrist and placed them behind his back to be cuffed.

J.D shook his head incredulity, tears swelled in his eyes as he tried to look around at the people that slowed traffic up in their vehicles to watch the scene. Perkins had stopped other pedestrians from walking while Jerald was being apprehended.

"You're goin' down, down for a long time pal. Yup bubba, right up the creek with the old fish so you can smell the real scales," Mc Greed whispered in J. D's ear.

"Why, God?" J.D. cried out.

"It wasn't God's decision, Jerald, it was your own," Perkins said reluctantly.

"That's right bud," Mc Greed added going through J. D's pockets pulling out a wad of money and the zipped pouch that carried the drugs.

"God didn't put a bundle of crack cocaine or specials, as you call it, in your pocket and tell you to sell it. Now you'll have to tell it to the judge my man, unless of course, you have some... information you'd like to share with us to help yourself out of this mess," Mc Greed initiated quietly.

"Man, I don't deal wit nobody like that!" J. D. exclaimed loudly, making sure the wrong person didn't assume that he was taking another option to get out of his situation.

"Ok, I'll call a car out," Mc Greed said to Perkins as he stood up slowly and glanced down at J.D. "

"Yeah, we need an evidence bag for his keys, money, and drugs. We also need a tow truck for that pretty car he has over there shining like a new born baby butt," Perkins said to Mc- Greed.

"I almost forgot about that beauty over there; you know that's a nice ride Jerald, or J. D.," Mc Greed reframed and smiled.

"Man, Jerald, all that you've gained illegally could have been earned legally with just a little education, hard work, and patience. You're still young, yet now you're going to spend half of your life behind bars for absolutely nothing that was worthwhile," Perkins said informatively as he kneeled next to Jerald, hoping on the possibility that J.D. would give them some valuable information.

"That's what drug dealers really ask for out of life," Mc Greed said wisely and added, "nothing'." Then he walked away towards the middle of the street, urging the observing pedestrians to move along as he attended his way to the surveillance van to make the necessary call he was ordered to do.

"You sure you don't have anything to offer?" Perkins asked J. D. for the last time.

"Get the fuck outta here," J.D. snapped angrily as tears rolled off his nose.

"Ok, have it your way, Kentucky-fried crack dealer," Perkins said then helped J.D. up on his feet.

Chapter 6

Preliminary Hearing – Phase 1

Wednesday, October 15th, 9:12am, Jerald Doley was escorted out a side door next to the judge's bench by a county sheriff. He was unable to walk one foot length after the other because of the thick, silver maniacal cuffed around his ankles. Jerald was dressed in an orange Atlantic County Jail jumpsuit, with hand cuffs tightly chained around his waist and wrist too. He was seated at the defense table next to a short, fat man who wore a dark blue, pin-striped suit, a red tie partly loosened around the neck, and a pair of wire framed spectacles; he was Jerald's public defender. He was clean shaved and had dark brown hair slicked to the left side of his head to cover a bald spot. Across from him, on the right side, was a young looking man, clean shaven, with dirty blond hair and brown framed glasses, and wearing a light gray suit. He was the prosecutor. He was reading through a pile of neatly stacked papers next to a large black briefcase and manila filing folder.

In the back of the court room, silently seated, was Jerald's heart- broken mother, at a distance. She was wearing black, pleated, khaki pants, a red silk blouse, and a padded suit jacket to match. Her black silky hair was pulled back in a bun. She watched her son enter the court room in an uncivilized garment jumper and shackled like a slave. Her stomach tightened in expectation of what was going to happen to her son. There was nothing she could do but reflect on what she tried to warn him about all the time. She knew nothing good would come out of this situation, but she prayed anyway because what was done was done. The best thing to do was to be there for him and keep it moving herself because she had two young daughters that still needed her attention.

The public defender sorted through his cluttered papers inside a faded brown brief case as the sheriff released his grip on Jerald's arm so he could sit. Jerald looked around the court room and noticed his mother over his right shoulder sitting in the corner behind him. They both exchanged painful expression and kept it brief.

"Okay... Mr. Doley, right?" the chunky man asked Jerald in a husky tone, disregarding eye contact.

"Yeah," Jerald answered slowly.

The short man pulled from his brief case a stack of papers. He sat silent for a second as he quickly flipped through the papers; he then looked at Jerald gave him a crooked smile to show a little humor. Jerald looked at him bitterly and shrugged.

"My name is Mr. Deam, Jerald," the chunky man introduced himself; "I am a public defender, and I was appointed to represent you on this matter. Do you have any questions?"

"Nah," Jerald replied sullenly, tightening his jaws.

"Qkay then, umm, I guess we can get the ball rollin'" Mr. Deam stated confidently.

He stood up, placed the stack of papers on the table, and walked over to the prosecutor's table. The public defender whispered to the prosecutor then returned to his seat. Sweat beaded on the top of the short man's forehead and ran to the bridge of his nose, causing him to push his glasses up to avoid slippage. The court room was silent; the few people that were present said nothing. The five-foot-six, blonde haired, forty- year- old stenographer entered the court room from behind the judge's bench, glanced quickly, and gave a slight smile at the bailiff. The prosecutor nodded to the bailiff, which indicated he was ready. The bailiff left the room through the door that Jerald and the six foot sheriff had entered. Bailiff Staton returned in seconds, Jerald's mother eased her way closer to her son too let him know she was there to support him. Jerald hesitantly turned around; he gave her a feeble smile, and she smiled encouragingly in return.

54

"All rise," announced the bailiff, "Court is now in session. The honorable Judge Mark Steinback is presiding."

The judge appeared from behind the bench dressed in a long black robe. The sixty- two year- old judge took a seat wearing wireless framed bifocals with a head full of white hair, and bristlely eyebrows.

"Please be seated," the judge asked kindly, "Mr. Herley," he called the attention of the prosecutor's to begin.

The prosecutor quickly stood to present his case.

"Yes, your honor. This case is State v.s. Doley, 2C; 35 under indictment 98-40—195. The defendant Jerald Doley, a.k.a J.D. has been charge with count one possession and counts two of intent to distribute narcotics to an undercover officer." He completed his opening argument and sat back down.

"Counsel," the judge referred to the public defender, "how does the defendant wish to plead?"

The public defender stood to address the court on the defendant's behalf.

"For the record your honor," Mr. Deam began, "My name is Jerry Deam; I was appointed by the state to represent Jerald Doley under 2C:35, indictment 98—40-195," he paused a split second so the middle aged court clerk of the court, who typed his last few words before the public defender began again.

"The defendant and I," Mr. Deam began again, looking at his papers, "haven't had a chance to go over the basis of the case. If we could, your honor, have a recess, I'd be gladly to have a plea for you and possibly more of what we'll contest against or perhaps agree with, thank you, your honor," he finished and took his seat.

The judge moved his eyes over the rim of his bifocal in a tedious way from Mr. Deam to the elegant looking prosecutor.

"Okay, counsel, a twenty minute recess," the judge ordered and slammed his gavel down once, and then he quickly left the bench to return to his chamber with the casually dressed stenography following steps behind.

Ms. Doley leaned over the wooden bench a little to ask Jerald if he was he alright.

"Yeah, I'm aw'ight," Jerald said sadly.

"Sheriff may I have a word with my client and his mother together?" Mr. Deam whispered to the six-foot man dressed in a light brown uniform that read "County Sheriff" on the shirt sleeves. He had dirty blond hair, pale skin, and a long, Irish nose.

"Sure you can Mr. Deam," the transit sheriff answered politely. "I'll have bailiff Staton retrieve him whenever you're finished or when court's over."

"Thank you sheriff," Mr. Deam said appreciatively and showed a friendly smile.

56

Jerald sat quietly; he felt uncomfortable with the manacles gripped tightly around his flesh. The sheriff walked over to the bailiff that looked to be in his late forties and spoke low. The bailiff nodded, said a few words, as the sheriff grinned on the way out the door. The prosecutor quickly walked out behind the sheriff not leaving any of his belongings behind. He nodded to bailiff Staton; the bailiff nodded in return. Mr. Deam turned halfway on his heels after he sorted the disorganized papers.

"Mrs. Doley is it?" he asked sharply in a conservative tone.

"Miss, that is, and, yes, the last name is Doley," she replied, correcting him sweetly.

"Sorry about that," he smirked foolishly.

"No problem," Ms. Doley answered politely.

"I'm Mr. Deam; I was appointed to represent your son on this matter."

"Of course," she said, gathering what she heard during the court introduction.

"Okay," he stated turning his attention to Jerald, not wanting to stare hard at the beautiful, well-dressed, black woman who sat in a conservative posture with the smell of "Polo" perfume lingering in th air.

"Well, Jerald, we're in a very tough situation here my man," Mr. Deam said. Jerald slowly looked at the

P.D. as tears swelled his eyes; he silently felt the distress his mother was experiencing.

"I have to speak with the prosecutor to see what we work can out or at least find out some factual evidence they have against you. The bailiff here is going to place you back into the holding tank until I return from talking to the prosecutor." The bailiff walked over to the defense table after hearing Mr. Deam finish his statement.

"He can't sit here with me and wait for you to get back?" Ms. Doley asked pleadingly.

"Sorry Ms .Doley, he's in the custody of the county now, if it was up to me I'd let him. He can't run anyhow, but they are the rules," he looked from Ms. Doley to his client.

"Come this way Mr. Doley," the bailiff said and gave Jerald a little room to stand before grabbing the back of his arm. Jerald sadly looked back at his mother while tears streamed down his cheeks.

"I love you mom," he managed to say.

"I love you to baby," Ms. Doley assured holding the aching pain in her chest as she watched the bailiff escort her son off like a captured insurgent.

"Jerald, I'll return in about ten minutes or so," Mr. Deam advised and stuffed the stack of papers inside his old-looking briefcase carelessly.

"Ms. Doley, I'll be right back; you sit tight and we'll see what we can do," Deam told her and stammered his chunky body out to the front entrance of the court room.

Ms. Doley slid back on the bench quietly, sniffed, and with a hand full of tissues dapped at the corners of each eye. She tried not to smear the eye liner she had taken hours to get right early that morning.

Chapter 7

Plea Hearing – Phase 2

At 9:47am, Mr. Deam short stepped his two hundred and forty-one pound body through the alarm entrance of the court house and handed the sheriff (who was seated at the tower) his beat up briefcase to avoid setting the alarm off.

"Thank you Sam," Deam said politely.

"My pleasure, Mr. Deam," the young sheriff responded respectfully.

Mr. Deam hurried his way to the court room; he peeped inside to see if anyone was there, and then he spun around and looked down each end of the court building.

"Where could you be Ms. Doley?" he mumbled to himself.

"Uhuh," he sighed. He consumed the air with his nose and picked up her familiar scent.

Deam paced his way down the opposite end of the court building. On his way he greeted a few lawyers and court employees and turned his face towards the young, black, thug looking males who may have been going to court for who knows what, he thought. He stopped at the entrance of the public lounge. Deam glanced around the large room set with four tables and chairs on each side, one soda and three snack machines, a built in coffee machine with a tea slot for option. He spotted Ms. Doley seated alone among the scattered people in the far corner. She was sipping on a Coke, staring blankly through the parted blinds hanging from the large oval windows. Mr. Deam huffed a little, out of breath, and cleared his throat before gathering his words.

"Ms. Doley," he called out mildly, holding his pointer finger up.

Ms. Doley looked around in wonder before seeing the public defender straining for her attention. She stood gracefully and slid the chair underneath the table respectfully and then walked over to one of the two trash cans prompted next to the snack machine and femininely tossed the half filled soda can in the recyclable. As she walked towards the P.D, she noticed his eyes glued to her breast.

"You would never get known of this, fatso," she thought silently.

The P.D. gave a tight smile and held the door open.

"Okay Ms. Doley, right" he began to say, but the dryness in his throat caused him to sound unprofessional.

"Excuse me," he coughed.

"I meant to say right this way Ms. Doley, but my voice went dry there."

"No problem," Ms. Doley replied with a smile, knowing what his focus was on.

"We have to get Jerald and discuss the seriousness of this case before the judge returns," he announced, readjusting his attention to business again.

Ms. Doley walked quietly on their way to the court room. Mr. Deam opened the door for her to enter before him.

"Thank you," she said.

"You're welcome," he replied, "I'll go ask the bailiff to bring Jerald back out."

Ms. Doley nodded and sat in the same seat. Mr. Deam placed his briefcase on the defense table and continued walking towards the door where bailiff Staton exited with Jerald. Deam stepped his full-figured through the door to see bailiff Staton seated behind a small desk gazing up at the ceiling no more than ten feet away.

"Bailiff," Mr. Deam called, interrupting the bailiff's quiet time. "Can you bring Jerald Doley back out now?" he requested.

"Sure, Mr. Deam," the bailiff replied, not amused at all.

The public defender re-entered the court room and informed Ms. Doley that Jerald was on his way out.

Bailiff Staton went down the far end of the wide hall that had several steel doors on each side, with a 4x6 inch double mounted, wire glass window on each door. The sound of keys echoed in the empty hall while the bailiff released them from his belt loop as he near the holding tank Jerald was in. He used a large brass key that looked like the ones used for an old castle to open the cell door. Jerald was seated straight up against the wall still shackled in manacles; his eyes were closed and didn't lift when the bailiff stood halfway in.

"Let's go Doley," bailiff Staton ordered.

Jerald moved slowly after partly opening his eyes; he walked out the steel tank stiffly.

"Hold on," the bailiff commanded authoritatively so he could lock the steel door back.

"Alright, you know the way," the bailiff said and allowed Jerald to take the lead, untouched.

Jerald shook his head and sucked his teeth as he made his way to the court room. Ms. Doley stared with sadness as her son was lead into the court room still bound, and suddenly held by the back of his arm.

"Oh, my baby, are you okay?" she cried silently

"I feel sick mom," Jerald replied feeling nauseous.

"Don't worry honey; you'll be alright, just pray baby, that's all, just pray, alright."

Mr. Deam interceded sharply, unable to hear anymore religious referencing.

"Jerald, here's the deal," he said, clearly, "they have you red handed on video and they have the drugs you were carrying. If you plead to the intent of distribution, which is count two here, and do not contest the property that was seized, which, however, you would lose regardless in that hearing, the prosecutor will come down on the original plea he had prepared to offer you and he'll dismiss the count one possession."

"What was the first plea?" Ms. Doley asked quickly.

"Twenty years, serve ten before parole eligibility," Deam answered indefinitely, then added, "oh, and school zone too."

"Nah, man, dat's too much!" Jerald exclaimed scarcely.

Mr. Deam looked at the frightened boy sympathetically for a second and puckered his lips as the sweat beaded down the side of his face.

"As I said, he'll come down under those conditions, if you take the plea."

The P.D. looked into Jerald's file after repeating the circumstances and pulled more paper work out the faded brief case.

"Now, for the forfeiture, let's see here," he pushed his glasses onto the bridge of his nose, and he tilted his head to one side for a better angle of the paper work.

"You had eight hundred dollars in cash on you, a bundle of crack cocaine, and a set of keys to a parked 1993 Ford Mustang. Jeeze' Jerald, that's, that's a heck of a lot relatively speaking of the drugs and money, with no employment, I take. And not to mention no driver's identification," Deam said dramatically.

"Oh, Jesus," Ms. Doley sighed, and reflected again on how she tried to warn Jerald so many times about that car.

"What's da' new plea? Jerald asked curiously, with resentment in his voice.

Without hesitation the public defender said, "Ten years with eighty five percent."

"I gotta do da' whole fifteen years?" Jerald shouted, bewildered.

"Well, calm down, not all of it, just a majority, which would be about eight and a half years," Deam calmly explained and shrugged, sitting with his elbows prompted on the brown shellac table; he stared from his client to the mother with a justified expression on his face.

"Good Lord!" Ms. Doley swore. "For God sake, you can't do better than that?" she questioned the public defender, emotionally.

"I can't do dat much time," Jerald cried. "I wish I had money for a paid lawyer," he added angrily.

Mr. Deam laid the file down with ease and tapped his beefy finger tips on the table a couple times before folding his hands together.

"At this point Jerald," he replied calmly, "a paid attorney couldn't get you a better deal under these circumstances," he advised; "I'm sorry to say, the new guidelines are in the prosecutor's favor one hundred percent and he's looking to seek the extended term for this being your second conviction of a second degree charge."

"What's an extended term?" Jerald asked confused.

"It's called doing double the amount of time you are being served," Deam answered and tried to fight back the sarcasm, offended by the doubtful remark made against him by J.D.

Jerald shook his head from side to side unable to lift his hands to his face as the tears of fear and hurt swell his eyes.

"I'm not even eighteen yet, and dis is only my second time," he cried wearily.

Ms. Doley sat silently as she had tried to process the news correctly but it was all too real at once to accept.

"That's the problem Jerald, it's your second time, so the prosecutor is looking to have you waved up as an adult; your birth date isn't far away, so it's likely that the judge will comply with the prosecutor's request and wave you," the P.D. explained with pleasure.

"Lord have mercy, I knew it, I knew it, Mr. Deam, you can't do nothing better for my son, he's still young?"

Mr. Deam gave Ms. Doley an empty look of despair.

"I'm afraid not Ms. Doley. If however, it was his first offense, I could probably do a lot better on the deal. The nature of this crime is extremely serious today, especially since that it's his second time. The system is cracking down on first time drug offenders as well as any other illegal substance offenders; more importantly, the distribution charge gives greater weight to their offense," the public defender explained seriously.

"Man," Jerald began, but was cut short by the bailiff.

"Mr. Deam, Judge Steinback is about to return."

"Thank you bailiff," the P.D replied.

"So, under those conditions or either trial it, and I warn you," he continued and pointed his finger at Jerald like a college professor, "the evidence that the prosecutor has on you will result in a definite loss if you trial it. Not to mention the plea agreement they tried to give you will be out and a new, severe sentence will be in. So it's up to you Jerald; I've taken drug cases to trial."

"Win any?" Jerald asked, thinking about the possibility.

"Not many, and this would certainly be a tough one," Deam replied, quickly.

Jerald closed his eyes slowly then reopened them he sensed a bad feeling about his public defender. It was difficult for him to formally express himself because of the lack of education. His mother had always told him that not staying in school or getting his GED would catch up to him, and so it had.

"I guess, I have to take da plea den," Jerald said with a tight face.

"You don't have to, but it would be a wise decision," Mr. Deam assured him.

"Mom," Jerald called and looked back to her for support.

Ms. Doley looked from the public defender to Jerald and exhaled at the no win situation.

"I suppose you have no other choice; that seems appropriate at this point baby," she spoke softly, and wished she didn't have to say those words to her child, her only son.

"Okay," Mr. Deam anxiously exclaimed, "just sign these few papers here." He slid the papers in front of Jerald, and pulled an ink pen out the top pocket of his suit jacket. "It's basically explains what I've simplified to you, which was giving you the circumstances of your case and plea agreement. I'll give your mother a copy once the judge signs them, and then we can move forward. You do understand Jerald?"

Jerald looked down at the cuffs on his wrist and wondered how he was going to sign some papers, when the shackles prohibited him to pull his arms but two inches away from his waist.

"I'll get the bailiff to release one of the cuffs for you," the P.D said, reading Jerald's body language.

"Nah, I got it," Jerald replied.

He stood up close to the table and inched the papers close to the edge near to him. Mr. Deam placed the pen near Jerald's hand which made it easier for Jerald to grab. He took the pen and scribbled his name, then Mr. Deam flipped through each page for him to complete.

"So you do understand everything I explained to you? Mr. Deam asked again, for clarity.

"Yeah, I guess so, I ain't stupid," Jerald answered tensely.

"Pray baby, every things gonna be alright," Ms. Doley said nervously as she sat close to the wooden divider that separated her from the defendant chair while her son signed fifteen years of his life to the system. The public defender tapped his other hand impatiently on the table.

"Alrighty," Mr. Deam said gratefully.

"The Judge will be entering any minute. I'll be right back, sit tight, you don't have to go anywhere, this time, until this part of the process is over."

The public defender gathered the papers quickly and hurried through the back entrance. Jerald and his mother exchanged painful expressions; they were unable to speak a word, now that the plea agreement was official. The bailiff remained posted against the wall four feet away from Jerald, until court was back in session. Minutes after the stenographer returned, bailiff Staton took his regular position next to the judge's bench, to announce the judge's entrance. Mr. Herley walked through the main entrance, disregarding eye contact with the defendant and his mother, and sat on the prosecution's side. Jerald eyed him violently and gritted his teeth angrily. Ms. Doley rolled her eyes, but paid more attention to her son's emotional turmoil. Mr. Deam entered the court room from the door he exited. He nodded to Mr. Herley in a pleasant way and slid a thin stack of papers next to the prosecutor as he assorted through the papers he carried. The public defender took his seat next to the defendant to prepare for the court proceeding.

"All rise," bailiff Staton announced.

"Please be seated," Judge Steinback ordered, "Mr. Deam, your client come to a decision?"

Jerald gave the public defender a hard stare as if he thought the judge knew the decision already. Mr. Deam stood in compliance to the court.

"Ah, yes, your honor, I've spoken to Mr. Herley and informed my client of the proposition," he said, and didn't look at the angry young man next to him.

"We have come to the decision to plead guilty your honor."

"So your client accepts Mr. Herley's plea agreement?" the judge asked again for reassurance.

"Yes, your honor," Mr. Deam replied assuredly, and then he took his seat.

"No, I can't do ten years, please give me a chance judge?" Jerald burst out loudly, tears swelled his eyes as he stared at the judge pitifully.

Judge Steinback slammed the gavel down twice from Jerald's outburst.

"So you don't want to take the plea, you'd rather go to trial?" the judge snapped irritably.

"No!" Jerald screamed out like a confused child.

Mr. Deam patted Jerald on the shoulder to calm him down as he stood to address the court.

"Your honor, we came to the decision of accepting the plea agreement, my apology for my client's outburst."

The judge huffed displeasingly, "Wise choice counselor."

"Please judge gimme a chance!" Jerald painfully repeated.

"Mr. Doley," the judge barked coldly, "you're out of order in my court room and you're most certainly old enough to know better. You had your chance when Judge Starks placed you on probation for the same offense, now you're here in my court room begging for another chance. You had your chance, now one more outburst like that or I'll hold you in contempt of court with a disorderly charge."

"I can't do dat much time, please!" Jerald stood in tears.

Ms. Doley stood and leaned over the rail and whispered for Jerald to calm himself. Mr. Deam tried talking some sense into his client, but the words didn't seem to penetrate.

"Bailiff," the judge requested.

Bailiff Staton quickly walked over to the defendant's table to detain Jerald and waited for further instructions.

"Please don't hurt my baby," Ms. Doley said sullenly.

"Jerald you better calm down or I won't be able to do nothing for you," the P.D. warned in a hushed way.

"Mr. Doley the court finds you in contempt and to be deterred back to Atlantic County Jail," the judge ordered before he slammed gavel.

The bailiff grabbed Jerald's arm tightly; the public defender shook his head, bizarrely unable to stop the judge's decision.

"Do you wish to proceed with this case Mr. Deam?" Judge Steinback asked. The public defender quickly jolted, thinking that he probably could get the judge to change the contempt, but not the disorderly conduct.

"Ahhh, yes, your honor, may I have a word with my client first?"

"Under the observation of the bailiff, yes, a five minutes recess," the judge announced slamming the gavel and once again disappeared behind the bench, with the stenographer on his heels, before the public defender could thank him. The prosecutor sat quietly as he went through papers, not giving the defense table any attention.

"Bailiff, can you escort my client to the conference room out here?"

Bailiff Staton complied and followed Mr. Deam to the conference room and kept a tight grip on Jerald's arm. Ms. Doley followed after them in silence with tears streaming down her face. They all entered a small room with a round wooden table and four wooden chairs right outside the hearing room. The bailiff stepped outside of the room, respectfully giving them privacy. Mr. Deam slammed a stack of papers onto the table, outraged.

"Jerald, you have to calm yourself down young man; this isn't no child circus here! I explained everything to you and your mother and you agreed to take the plea. There is no more that can be done except to withdraw from the plea and taking it to trial," he snapped angrily, but spoke conservatively.

"I'm sorry, I can't do it, I don't wanna take it to trial either." Jerald whined, feeling his stomach touch the floor and heat rising in his throat at a hundred degrees.

The P.D. took his glasses off and pulled out a handkerchief to wipe the sweat off his forehead and glasses.   .

"Well, Jerald, you signed the papers already," he said calmly, then continued, "now you'll have to sit in the county jail until sentencing. I was going to see if I could get you out on bail on your on recognizance, but you obviously screwed that up."

"Can you please try anyway, Mr. Deam?" Ms. Doley asked, pleadingly.

"I'm sorry Ms. Doley," he said, and placed his glass's back on to better see her; "Jerald really upset the judge with that outburst; there's no way he'll go for it now."

The bailiff knocked twice before entering and announced, "You have one minute, Mr. Deam."

"Thank you," the P.D. replied, "we'll go forward with the hearing so we can get it over with. We don't need to repeat this process over again, sentencing is the next step, and the judge is not going to waste any more time when he feels it's already been wasted."

"Wait a minute," Ms. Doley said, "why couldn't he get bail before?"

"He did Ms. Doley, but the two undercover police officers testified at the probable cause hearing, which Jerald didn't have to attend and the judge revoked his bail immediately, believing that he could be a flight risk," the public defender explained.

"A flight risk, why wasn't I notified?" she questioned, confused.

Mr. Deam put his hands up in defense.

"Ms. Doley, I'm fresh on the case. I have no idea," he turned to his client, "Jerald wasn't you issued a bail prior to your arrest?"

Jerald kept his head down embarrassed, "Yeah," he mumbled.

"What was your bail?" Deam asked.

"Fifty thousand, no ten percent, no bail bonds, dey said."

"There's your answer Ms. Doley," the public defender said, feeling he escaped hot water.

"Okay, let's go Mr. Doley," the bailiff said to Jerald waiting to get a grip on the convict's arm.

"I'm still here baby, don't worry," Ms. Doley assured Jerald on their way back into the court room.

"Why? Why me?" Jerald cried under his breath resentfully while the bailiff decided to check the cuffs on his wrist, waist, and ankles before seating him at the defense table.

"Alright, be seated," the bailiff ordered Jerald then walked behind the judge's bench to see if Judge Steinback was ready to appear. Bailiff Staton immediately returned while everyone sat back in their seats for the rest of the hearing.

"All rise," Bailiff Staton announced.

"Be seated," Judge Steinback ordered harshly with a hardened expression across his face, "Mr. Deam, your decision please."

The public defender stood at attention and noticed the serious expression on the judge's face. There was no way he would be able to convince the judge to release his client on his own recognizance, he thought.

"Continue with the proceeding, with the respect of the court your honor," the public defender answered nervously.

"Mr. Herley," the judge called to speak.

"Your honor, since the defendant has a prior conviction of distribution, the state is requesting the extended term. I am sure Mr. Deam explained that to his...his client, as well, your honor, so we don't have any more surprises that may delay this matter," Herley said tediously, and sat.

"Mr. Deam does your client understand the meaning of this imposition regarding the extended term?" Judge Steinback asked.

The public defender stood again to answer carefully, hoping to sooth the tension the judge held towards his client.

"I, umm, explained with the best of my knowledge, your honor. I truly believe that my client, umm, comprehends the significance of this matter."

"Mr. Doley, please stand," the judge requested.

Jerald stood reluctantly with his mother whispering quietly for him to stay calm.

"Mr. Doley," the judge began, "young men like you need to learn that this society today is not tolerating drug involvement any longer. There are no reasons why you should think of reverting back to your life of selling drugs again after this experience."

"I'm sorry Judge," Jerald exclaimed quickly, his eyes wide and searching for leniency.

"Being sorry does not cut it, Mr. Doley," the judge replied hastily, then continued in an abrupt manner, "We, as the system have to show people like you that there are no more three time deals. You have to be considered as an example to society today. I believe that the state Supreme Court is too lenient on drug offenders," Judge Steinback stated in a lecturing tone, with a brief pause to browse through papers.

"Here you have no education, no employment history, and you use drugs for your personal preference, to top off your situation."

Jerald stood in silence with his shoulders slouched with a despairingly look of exhaustion on his face. He stared blankly ahead of him and listened vaguely to what the judge had said.

"Mr. Doley, you're a young man. This plea agreement is ostensibly sufficient for you. I hope that your family and some positive people in your community will help you next time if you happen to come into to such a problem ever again. Mr. Herley," the judge turned his attention to the prosecutor, "You can file that motion for an extended term now at this time."

The prosecutor stood and respectfully replied, "Of course, your honor."

"We had a lateness problem once too many times from the prosecution," the judge added.

"Sure, your honor, understood."

"Mr. Doley are you sure you understand your decision in this matter?" Judge Steinback asked, uncertain that the defendant understood his situation because of his comprehension level; for a better word, his lack of education.

"Yeah," Jerald responded clearly.

"Are you being coerced or threatened in any way to make this decision?" the judge questioned.

"Umm, no"

"Mr. Herley, do you have a closing statement?" the judge asked.

"No, your honor," Herley answered.

"Mr. Deam?" the judge called.

"Uh, yes, your honor if I may, umm... I would like to request that my client be released on his own recognizance under your honor's condition that he be placed on a twenty hour home device with the supervision of his mother and have an every five hour call check to the proper authority that's in charge of the monitoring system?"

"Denied," the judge replied quickly and coldly, "anything else counsel?"

"That will be all, your honor, thank you," the P.D. said.

"Alright," Judge Steinback spoke, "for the record - State vs. Doley 2C:35 under indictment 98-40-195 count one possession and count two possessions with intent to distribute. The defendant pleaded guilty on both counts and fully understands the condition of this plea agreement," he said and scribbled something down on the paper he was reading from. "Sentencing will be held on December 17th at 9 am," the judge officially announced, then slammed the gavel down once. "Court is adjourned."

The judge stood, took the file with him, and exited behind the bench once more. Jerald looked at his mother and stood watching the tears of pain roll down her face. The bailiff politely escorted Jerald out of the court room. Mr. Deam tried to inform Jerald that he will be in touch with him before sentencing day.

"I love you mom," Jerald said, cutting the public defender's words off.

"I love you too baby; be strong."

Chapter 8

Sentencing – Final Phase (3)

Thursday, December 17th, 9am sharp, Jerald Doley was escorted into the court room, shackled tightly around the waist with both wrists and ankles in cuffs, like a savage beast, and dressed in the same orange Atlantic County jumper. In the back of the large court room sat his mother, alone, dressed like an executive woman. Jerald immediately noticed her; he had expected her to be present. Ms. Doley gave him a warm smile for support as he was lead to the defense table. Mr. Deam burst into the court room entrance. He appeared ten pounds heavier. He wore a dark blue, bloody red, pin-striped suit, with a black silk tie, and a pair of black comfortable loafers that leaned to the side like a ship turned overboard. At the table parallel the defendant, in a casual, neatly pressed, dark gray suit was seated Mr. Herely, seeming to be prepared for the final occasion.

The court stenographer entered the room from behind the judge's bench and sat at her typing area, quickly, as usual. Bailiff Staton resided at his regular standing post and waited to announce the judge's appearance. The sheriff nodded at the public defender as he remained positioned silently next to the defendant. He then exited the court room sending a coy smile at the bailiff after Mr. Deam acknowledged his nod. Ms. Doley moved up closer to the defense side. A second later, detective Perkins and officer Mc Greed entered the court room casually dressed and clean shaved. Both took a seat at the back of the court, concealing their presence.

"Is everything alright, baby?" Ms. Doley asked Jerald softly.

He nodded in response. The public defender turned to speak quietly to Ms. Doley.

"Oh, hi, Ms. Doley, I didn't see you sitting there when I came in."

"Hello," she replied, considerately.

The public defender took out a large stack of papers from his black briefcase, which looked more professional than the beat up, brown one he carried last hearing.

"Well," he exhaled, specifically at his client, "the judge should be entering any minute. I thought I was running late today."

Jerald didn't seem to be moved by the public defender's extra information. He sat silently looking forward, unable to comprehend this detrimental experience once again and, most importantly, the pain he had caused his mother for not listening to her wisdom. She warned him day-in and day-out about his illegal activities, which he thought nothing about until now.

"All rise," the bailiff trumpeted, "the honorable Judge Mark Steinback is presiding."

The judge curled his black robe around his body so he could be seated comfortably behind the immense wooden bench.

"Please be seated," he said pleasantly and looked in the direction of the prosecutor.

"Mr. Herley, are you ready to present your extended-term brief on this matter or have you not filed it yet?"

The prosecutor stood firmly twisting his ink pen through his boney fingers, feeling confident that the case was a victory.

"Sure, your honor," he replied boldly and continued; "because of the nature of the defendant's crime, the State offered the defendant a ten year sentence with an eighty-five percent serving time under the condition that the defendant accepts the plea agreement. We will dismiss count one possession under the condition that all properties and monies are seized. The State has filed its motion for an extended term as a result of this being the defendant's second conviction. Mr. Deam and I went over the significance of the motion; therefore, the sufficiency of the case still stands firm." The prosecutor ended and then sat.

The public defender stood quickly to object argumentatively before the prosecutor could come up with any other condition.

"Your honor, my client has accepted the prosecution's plea agreement under those conditions which the prosecutor has stated. However, the litigation of an extended term is severe, due to the fact that my client only has one prior offense. He served probation for the offense as a juvenile and completed it successfully. Moreover, this extended term should not be imposed as relevant criteria. Based on the given information, the sentencing itself should not be extended for a first time adult conviction. The eighty-five percent my client has agreed to serve should be all that is mandated."

"Mr. Deam," the judge began harshly, "your client has accepted the plea offer, which cannot be more appropriate than it is," he continued angrily. "The extended term is mandatory and pertinent for the state to impose on second time offenders, whether adult or juvenile, in this case. His juvenile conviction wasn't considerably far from this conviction and it is also cited under the Brimage law. The prosecutor has consulted with you on this matter; therefore, your argument is impertinent and unnecessary, and all motions for appeals are on your time."

"Yes, your honor," the public defender respectfully submitted.

"Mr. Herley," the judge called with implication in his voice.

"Nothing more your honor; thank you," the prosecutor said assuredly, with a triumphant smile across his lips.

"Very well then," Judge Steinback answered. "Mr. Doley, will you stand please."

Jerald gave the judge a blank stare, but complied reluctantly with his request.

The judge beaded his eyes a little through his clear wireless spectacles, while his eyebrows hovered over the frames.

"Mr. Doley, how old are you?" the judge asked.

"Seventeen," Jerald answered.

"Mr. Doley, are you presently on parole or probation of any kind?"

"No," the defendant replied, annoyed.

"Sir, are you satisfied with your attorney's representation?"

"Yeah," Jerald said, and cut his eye at the short chunky man, then looked back at the judge.

"Mr. Doley, I need you to speak up," the judge ordered.

"Yes!" Jerald answered.

The judge became a little agitated with the defendant's sarcasm, but didn't show that it had any effect on him.

"Mr. Doley, do you understand that if you decide to appeal this sentence on some other grounds other than what you have pleaded guilty to that the State can, and possibly will, withdraw from your plea bargain, reinstate all charges, and everything will start over again?"

Jerald looked at his public defender before answering. The public defender gave him a cohesive look and slightly nodded his head.

"Yes," Jerald unwillingly answered, wishing he could take the plea back and get a paid attorney for a better sentence.

"Okay, Mr. Doley, on October the third, were you on the corner of New York and Pacific Ave in Atlantic City?"

"Yes."

"Did you distribute narcotics to an undercover police officer?"

"Yes," Jerald answered timidly.

"How many bags?" the judge asked stiffly.

"Like...five."

"What actually was it?" Judge Steinback asked, pointedly.

"Crack," the defendant replied.

"Crack Cocaine, you mean?" the judge questioned for clarification.

"Yes," Jerald mumbled.

The judge was unmoved; his reputation of sentencing young black men to prison for the solicitation of illegal substances was well-known; Jerald's case was no different.

"You can have a seat now, Mr. Doley," the judge told him and motioned the prosecutor.

"Alright," he paused a second, "Counsel, do you have anything else further on this matter?"

"No, your honor, I believe that satisfies the factual basis of this case.

The judge directed his question to the public defender. "Mr. Deam, do you have anything else?"

The P.D. stood his short body straight up to reply.

"Uh, no, no, your honor, that, that'll be all," he stuttered.

The judge reckoned that since there were no concluding arguments from either the defense or prosecution, he would move on. Judge Steinback began to recite the final declaration of sentencing to end the hearing.

"In light of the statement made by the defendant, I will accept the guilty plea. It is being made knowingly, intelligently, and voluntarily, with sufficient understanding of the legal sequences together with adequate factual basis."

Jerald bowed his head and reflected while the judge was speaking of the day of his apprehension. The day that pretty, petite Shemika warned him about his drug dealing. *"You going to get yours one day"* he remembered her saying clearly. The judge's voice remained vague as he dwelled on her statement, as if she was the cause of his down fall.

"That I hear by deter the defendant over to the Atlantic County Department of Correction."

That part of the judge's speech jolted Jerald out of his daydream like a slap across the face. The bailiff was initiated by the judge's closing statement to detain Jerald before court was adjourned. The judge's speech continued, "With a fifteen year sentence in terms of completing eighty five percent firmly."

"Counsels, is that all?" the judge asked.

"Yes, thank you, your honor," the prosecutor half-stood to say.

"Yes, thank you, your honor," the public defender followed.

"All paper work to the clerk…court is now adjourned." The judge hammered the gavel down once before swiftly leaving the bench.

Jerald stood aghast as bailiff Staton gripped his arm tightly. Jerald looked towards his mother slowly as tears fell from the corner of his eyes. He blinked repeatedly, noticing the disappointment on her face as she fought anxiety, since his arrest. The bailiff motioned Jerald to walk in the direction of the door where they entered the court room. Jerald began to shake his head from side to side wildly. The public defender avoided further confrontation as Jerald was lead out the court.

"No!" Jerald cried out loud in fear of imprisonment, leaving an eerie echo in the court room.

Ms. Doley stood fearfully for Jerald as she thought about him entering an uncivilized environment, yet leaving a dangerous lifestyle from the streets, where death was inevitable. She could only think of the three places young black men end up when dealing with illegal activities: jails, institutions, or six-feet under.

Detective Perkins and Mc Greed exchanged hand daps in victory as they listened to the final sentencing. It was a chapter ended in the detectives' quest of a drug bust; a new chapter began in Jerald's life, one that would change his life.

Chapter 9

Lock - up

On January 20th, 1997, Trenton State Prison, Jerald was led by two correction officers; his hands were cuffed behind his back, he wore white State boxers and a pair of State shower shoes, and he was put into an eight by ten foot cell after having a long, restless, uncomfortable stay in the county jail.

"In there and turn around, so I can take off the cuffs," one of the two officers ordered.

"Yo, don't be treatin' that kid like he's an animal," a prisoner yelled out in the next cell, with his body pressed against the steel bars.

"Shut up Roach, before you get some more lock-up time," the short, stubby correctional officer retorted harshly, in a country accent.

"On what charge?" the prisoner rebuked.

"I'll make one up," the officer snapped and walked closer to the prisoner's cell. The officer began to foam at the corner of his mouth as he shouted at the top of his lungs at the prisoner. He was never fond of prisoners ever since he became a correctional officer seven year earlier. He hated black people even more; ever since he was a little fat, one tooth, freckle- faced kid growing up in Mississippi on his parents' farm he attended all of his father's Klan rallies.

"Now mind your goddamn business boy or you'll be next!" he said angrily, with fiery eyes.

The other officer closed the cell door Jerald had been placed in and ordered him to back up against the bars so he could release the cuffs off his wrists. The prisoner next cell, Rick, a.k.a. "Roach," continued to dispute the officer's threatening statement.

"Do what you got to champ; I have nothin' to lose," Roach said sarcastically and paused a second.

"Alright Rick, chill out," the tall, slim, rookie officer advised.

"I'll be ya witness Rick!" another prisoner exclaimed a cell down.

"What you should be is not in here, now keep blowing shit, badass," the stubby officer barked.

"Are you okay kid?" Rick asked Jerald, curiously.

"Yeah," Jerald replied quietly as he scarcely curled up on the naked bunk.

"You have rights in here if you didn't know," Rick informed.

"Not in here you don't. Now shut the fuck up, asshole," stubby officer Briggs yelled angrily.

"I have the fuckin' rule book," Rick barked back and scowled at the two officers with hate.

"Ricky, you've been in here long enough to know whose word sticks around here," the rookie officer said calmly. Blanks was a thin, five- foot-eleven, clean shaved, conservative officer who dressed neatly. He had been raised in upstate New York by both parents, who were Republicans. His mother taught him to respect people for who they were, regardless of their race, creed, and color. But here he was a first year rookie partnered with a bigot officer that would eventually rub off on him, yet to come.

"I said I'm okay," Jerald sat up so he could be heard clearly.

"Good boy," Briggs stated with a sinister grin; "see, he knows and you've been here long enough to know convict. Apparently you're still stuck on the unchangeable; you must still be fuckin' brain dead."

"Whatever pig," Rick replied.

"What's that?" Briggs asked and moved closer t Rick's cell with one hand gripped to the electric shocker clipped to his waist side.

"That's what I thought," Briggs said, getting no feedback from the prisoner.

"When am I get'n blankets, and clothes and shit?" Jerald asked standing up near the bars.

"When the trustee comes around," Blanks answered wisely.

"When's dat?" Jerald fired back.

"What did the officer say?" Briggs shouted as he moved towards Jerald's cell with his hand still on the electric gadget.

"Wait," Briggs added, "this ain't no damn holiday inn."

"The trustee should be around in a little while kid," another prisoner said on the opposite side of Jerald's cell.

"Yeah, the- know- it- all brothers got all the answers you need," Briggs stated sarcastically and pivoted before walking away. "Just don't try to know too much or you'll end up not knowing anything at all, got me?"

"That's right Doley," Blanks added before he walked behind his senior officer. "Try following the guy in the cell over there." He pointed to a Caucasian prisoner two cells down from Jerald's, lying quietly.

"He's a pig too," Rick uttered abruptly, referring to the Caucasian inmate.

The two officers walked away down the dim hall, leaving the prisoners in distress.

"Whatever dude!" Saul, the Caucasian inmate, retorted and broke the silence.

"I bet he ain't got that much time," Rick stated.

"I got enough time. I'm not a career criminal," replied the inmate.

"You don't have to be a career criminal, you a criminal and ya ass is in here," remarked Ali, the prisoner on the other side of Rick's cell.

"Call it what you want man!" the white inmate said nonchalantly.

"I call it how I see it, dude!" Ali responded.

"How old are you little brotha?" Rick asked Jerald.

"Seventeen," Jerald answered.

"Damn, you young as hell; they must of waved you as an adult."

"Yeah, I guess so," Jerald replied, still in a state of obscurity.

"Man," Ali whistled.

"What's ya name kid?" Rick asked, avoiding the irrational behavior from his cellmate, Ali.

"J.D.," Jerald answered.

"First time down?" Rick questioned again.

"In prison, yeah," Jerald slowly answered as he exhaled anxiety.

"It's not bad," the white inmate interrupted.

"Speak for ya self; you need to mind ya fuckin' business too, you probably only got slapped on the wrist like the rest of you crack-asses do." Ali snapped at the white inmate.

"Isn't that the way the system works?" Rick mentioned objectively.

"Whatever dude; I'm still in prison," Saul exclaimed boldly."

"You haven't been here that long," Rick protested, shaking the cell gate with both hands.

"Man, this shit is corny," J. D. whined as he became irritated with the situation he'd gotten himself into. He noticed the smell of urine mixed with funk smoldering the air. This was a beginning of the end, he thought. His big spacious queen size bed, the stereo system, the nice car, the weed he was polluting his lungs with, had all been like a good dream turned into a nightmare. No prison was a dream he thought; the dirt, the darkness, and the cold feeling behind those prison walls were not something he wanted to experience as a reality.

"Listen kid, J.D. I mean, I don't know the situation with you, but hold strong little brotha, ya life ain't over yet," Rick tried to encourage sincerely.

"Seventeen, jeeze," Ali mimicked gravely.

"Yeah, sure,' Jerald replied to Rick's advice. *You'll see reality one day*, Shemika's words rang in his head.

At that moment Rick became annoyed with Ali's mocking.

"Yo 'ock, stop fuckin' mimickin' people all the time. That shit is gettin' on my fuckin' nerves; that ain't real, that's bullshit."

"Ey, man, we gonna know about each other sooner or later," Ali replied jokingly.

"Not now," Rick said.

J. D's mind popped back to the present situation after hearing the other two prisoners' exchange of words.

"It's aw'ight," J.D. insisted.

"That's not how I see it, family," Rick said sharply, pissed off.

"You always seein' shit ya way Rick," Ali suddenly shouted, and felt the tension coming from Rick's cell.

"That's because I'm able to rationalize with time in the inside. This is no fuckin' game niggra."

"Who said it was?" Ali disputed angrily.

"I only sold crack to a cop," J.D. voluntarily gave in. The lock-up wing went completely quiet for about a minute; even the rats and other rodents put their ears to the floor to hear the youngster speak.

The prison system had been a society in itself for many years. It had just gotten worst in the mid-nineties. The inmates had become sex addicts with one another, institutional violators', and extreme gossipers. They craved to hear what was happening on the streets; most importantly, they made it a priority to know who owed who what in the cell next door, as if it was making their time in prison go by faster. But as the saying goes, "Misery likes company," whatever sounded miserable and whoever lived miserable made a lot of the prisoners feel good about themselves because of it.

"Heea vyyy," Ali remarked, breaking the silence.

"Will you shut the fuck up for once with the drama Ali. You be trippin' on some dumb shit," Rick snapped, hearing his words echo off of the empty walls.

"Ey, this cat in here for drugs too; I don't know if he really sold to a cop, so he said," Ali stated, trying to alter Rick's attention from his senseless behavior.

"What you mean, so I said?" Saul said, knowing that Ali was referring to him.

"I told you guys more than yous should already know."

"I bet!" Rick said sharply.

The cell block became instantly quiet again and every man seemed subdued in his own thoughts. Saul, however, sucked his teeth and waved Rick's remark off, annoyed and mumbling under his breath. J. D. exhaustedly curled back up on the naked bunk and felt hopeless from his captivity. The other two prisoners Rick and Ali stood against the cell gate with their arms out through the bars in a relaxed position. Suddenly the prisoners heard keys jingle and muffled words at the end of the hall.

"Okay," the voice said.

A Spanish inmate walked down the wing and greeted the familiar faces that had been separated from population for some time. He approached Jerald's cell dressed in brown khaki attire with his shirt buttoned to the neck.

"Hey, papi, you the new guy bro?" he asked Jerald.

"Yeah," Jerald replied sitting up on the cold, uncomfortable bunk slowly.

"I have sheets and blanket for you. Mess won't be for another hour and a half," the Spanish prisoner told Jerald.

"What about some clothes?" Jerald stressed.

"You don't get no clothes in lock-up papi, except for a dumper, which I can't tell you when these pigs will send it down," the Spanish inmate answered sincerely. "You musta messed up in the county bro to come straight to lock," he added as he handed Jerald two stained sheets that were supposed to have been white, and a thin gray, wool blanket that could barely cover his body.

"Thanks yo," Jerald said and accepted the material through the bars.

"My name is Jose, papi. I'm what you call a trustee for lock-up and for my housing unit in population. Dat means I get to run around the buildin' and get things for guys' dat need stuff and the pigs too. Just a little movement, that's all."

"Shit, with all that time you got I," Ali began to say, but was cut short by Rick's harsh words.

"Why do you always come out ya fuckin' face ignorantly, Ali, damn, shut up sometimes. I don't understand ya reason man, damn."

"What?" Ali replied naïve.

"I don't mind," Jose said humbly; "he's not too far from me with prison time anyway. I've known Ali for awhile now and he's no harm," he explained, looking from Rick to J.D.

"I know Jose, but that's not the point. Ali's always mimickin' or makin' stupid remarks; he knows betta than that bullshit."

"He definitely does," Saul commented, hoping to piss Ali.

"Shut the fuck up snitch!" Ali snapped angrily at the Saul.

"Prove it jump man," Saul challenged, unfazed by Ali's temper.

"You lucky we can't get outta these cells cracka jack," Ali threatened with hate.

99

"I got ya cracker, jump man, so get it straight dude."

"You a lucky fuckin white boy, I m tellin' you," Ali fired and paced back and forth in the tight cell.

The white inmate faded out in his own thoughts again and considered the argument as victorious on his behalf. Jose looked at J.D., shrugged his shoulders and never made a suggestive comment about the two other prisoners' verbal battle.

"So what's ya name bro?" Jose asked Jerald.

Jerald replied by giving Jose his a.k.a and tried to accept his present circumstance, but he still found his situation scant and inhumane.

"Since you on the same track Jose, we minds well have a group session," Ali started to cool his temper towards Saul because he knew he may never get to come in physical contact with him.

"You'd like that wouldn't ya?" the white prisoner remarked. Ali was a dark, chocolate complexioned, frail built, unshaved black man with a woolly, salt and pepper, miniature afro. Ali stuck one of his boney arms through the bars of his cell, using his pointer finger, and violently shouted in anger as he foamed at the mouth like a pit-bull ready for a match.

"Up yours, you rat-ass bastard, cracka mothafucka. I'll show you a fuckin' groupie, pussy- ass bitch," he spat.

Jose rubbed one hand over his face and listened to the name calling Ali blazed at the white inmate. He kept himself humble because that was the kind of man he had conditioned himself to be over the years he'd been incarcerated.

"Okay," he continued to explain to J.D. after the two prisoners calmed down, "to let you know where you at, dese is the lock-up for all da disciplinary prisoners. Zat means any of us who catches a charge, you done your lock-up time, den you see a committee that's called Classification. Dey classify you to a unit in population or to another prison. If they think that you are too much trouble to be in here, you'll go to ad-seg if that's what your charges carry."

"Then what's the snitch doin' in here?" Ali exclaimed sarcastically, referring back to the six foot, red- headed, young looking Caucasian prisoner, five cells down from his, towards the front.

"To watch your ass, jump man," replied Saul.

"Ain't shit you can watch here boy except for this big black man dingo, pussy," Ali said.

"You do need monitorin' Ali you very noisey bro," Jose said, trying not to sound prejudice.

"Thank you Jose," Saul exclaimed, feeling lofty from Jose's statement, which he felt supported his argument.

"There you go Ace, I ain't even sayin' nuttin'," Ali said to avoid conflict with someone that serves his meals on wheels daily.

"We minds well talk about our situation; we up in the big house now, I mean what the fuck," Ali said suggestively.

"See," Jose began, referring to Ali's condition of wanting to know everybody's business.

"You sure you want to expose the truth about yourself, jump man?" Saul remarked.

"I have no problem bro; maybe someone can learn from my story and pass it on once they re-integrate back into society," Jose expressed earnestly.

"Yeah, that'll be a story to sympathize with cause jumpin' from tree to tree is definitely not a story to tell kids," said the red- headed inmate, referring to Ali.

"If we was on the other side of these bars you wouldn't talk that shit cause you'd experience a lot more than this, fagot," Ali said, seriously.

"You certainly would bro, he's not tellin' no lie about that," Jose agreed, implying that the Saul's mouth was too big to escape population unharmed.

"What's the other side like," J. D. asked Jose curiously after he made his bunk.

"That's part of why I'm in this rat- ass hole over here," Rick finally spoke out standing a good five-foot-eleven with a bald head, and brown skin, after hearing

102

the impertinent argument amongst the other two convicts.

"Damn, brotha Rick finely speaks from the dead," Ali stated jokingly.

Rick avoided the comment and fell silent for a second, reflecting on memories of being back at home in Compton.

"If you not down with a gang or a thorough homie wit some protection," Jose said as he shook his head shook seriously, "then you'll have some real problems bro; it's no joke out in population. Dis place is like, uncontrolled dangerous zone when it want to be. And trust me bro, it's like that a lot, mainly when the pigs not watchin' jokers be snappin' on some other shit. Dat's why it's good to have protection," he encouraged staring at Jerald critically, "like a crew bro, you know?"

"But I'm only in here for a drug charge," Jerald proclaimed innocently.

"Don t matter now bro, you in here," Jose advised with a hand gesture and sternness that indicated there was nothing positive that could have been resolved from the situation regardless.

"Listen, young blood," Ali began, like an old gangster that been doing prison time for years, "I'm in lock-up for assault cause I got jumped by some niggas cause they heard I was in prison for havin' a rape charge on my jacket. I mean it ain't no secret; the mothafuckin' pigs put it out there for shit to happen to me. Dey didn't like the real shit I talked to them. Anyway," Ali continued as the other prisoners listened with disbelief, "I knifed one of them fag-ass-niggas after I got my shit togetha. I have mothafuckin' thirty-five years to do with nineteen in," he stressed, seriously. "I should be seein' parole soon. I'm expectin' a hit…fuck it…that's the way shit works in here. You can't trust no mothafucka out there in population. I've been to four prisons since I've been down and dey all the same no love in the inside and damn sure no love on the outside. Papi here is tellin' no bullshit; you gotta watch ya fuckin'back, or it will get the fuck chopped soons you turn ya head."

"Do you think you rehabilitated yourself since you been down?" Jose asked Ali.

"Depend on what you mean by rehabilitation," Ali replied. "They'll probably max my ass anyway 'cause I've been in and out of lock-up, and ad-seg, and other prisons since my bid started. But I did get more program certificates then a little bit. These mothafuckas don't care doe believe dat."

"Sure you do and you can count on the max too," Saul said sarcastically.

"I wish I could get a hold of you, little bitch," Ali said viciously and gripped the bars tight with anger. "You wouldn't be poppin' that bullshit for sure," he added.

"I'm in prison for murder robbery while robbing a convenient store," Jose confessed earnestly to J.D., positioned directly in front of his cell.

"I got thirty years to life, bro," Jose continued, "I got fifteen in, dat's how I got the trustee job." He paused a second, and looked down both ends of the dimmed hall to make sure the officers weren't close enough to hear their conversation before continuing. "I haven't been in trouble in the system for thirteen years. I get gray hairs bro dreamin' about freedom so I just live day by day. Dis shit is no place to be bro especially if you got kids out there. Bein' young like you, a lot of guys is go'n try you quick to see where you heart at, so you have to be prepared."

"They definitely will young brotha," Rick agreed whole-heartedly. "I suppose I have to tell a story to about my life, huh, Ali?" Rick stated sharply.

"Why not?" Ali responded quickly.

"That shits real easy for you to say," Rick shot back.

"I have a hundred and twenty five years for double murder and kidnappin'. Don't even ask Ali, you don't need to know.

"I'm not sayin' nothin'," Ali replied.

"I'll never see the outside world again or the family I once had." Rick took a short breath and kept his composure; "I'm up here in lock-up for a double-o-two…attempted murder on some bitch- ass niggras. Now I'm waitin' to be transferred the hell up outta here to ad-seg where I can get the fuck away from these pigs in here that's all."

105

"Damn," J.D. said under his breath, devastated to hear the prisoners' testimonies.

"Man," J.D. huffed again, "well y'all know my story, sellin' drugs to an undercover cop...I got fifteen years wit a eighty-five-percent. Plus they said somethin' about seekin' dat extended term."

Ali whistled dramatically again, "Damn, they ain't playin' fair out there on the drug laws today."

"No way bro, I watch da news ery day. All dey talk is drug busts and some crime watch people to help stop it," Jose said informatively.

"Yeah, snitch you in here for drugs right?" Ali said to Saul.

"First of all dude, my name is Saul, not snitch, and what I'm in here for is better than what you are Jump man."

"If I could touch you bitch- ass," Ali voiced intensely.

"I didn't sell to no cop anyway," Saul said.

"Don't matta mothafucka, drugs is drugs, you broke the law," Ali replied.

"That's the way is seems," Jose interceded, "but the law is much more severe on some drug offenses den others."

"I'm in here for fighting a gang member in population," Saul said, trying to change the topic about drugs.

"We ain't talkin' bout bein in fuckin' lock-up fool," Ali said authoritatively.

"You were the one that was gettin' extorted?" Jose asked Saul.

"Not extorted, they were just taking my things."

"Extortion motha fucka. Ain't no such shit as just takin' ya things in prison; extortion is what it was, so extortion is what it is," Ali stated with clarity.

"Dude whatever; I'll be outta here any day to go to a drug program so who gives a fuck."

"How much time you got?" Jose asked Saul curiously.

"A five with a three year stip'," Saul said like it was a large incarceration sentence.

"That's it bro?" Jose said surprisingly with a frown.

"Tell'em why, white boy," Ali shouted.

Saul seemed reluctant to give up more information than he had told to the listening prisoners. He sucked his teeth before speaking again and pretended like nothing mattered.

"I was selling LSD and got charged for manufacturing heroin, but it wasn't much," he said.

"What?" J.D. shouted in disbelief and jumped off the bunk to stand closer to the gate.

"Yeah, young blood, a slap on the wrist," Ali commented sarcastically.

Jose did the famous Ali whistle and shook his head in disbelief himself.

"Yo papi, I gotta roll, pigs comin'. I'll be back later to feed; we'll kick it den."

Jose then walked off down the narrow hall where a correctional officer had waved for him to leave out. The rest of the prisoners became silent as they heard muffled words and jingling keys moving closer in their direction.

"Saul Furley," the approaching officer called, "pack up, New Hope drug program transportation's here to pick you up."

"I'm ready," the red- headed prisoner said anxiously.

"Alright, turn around so I can put these cuffs on you."

"Through the bars?" Saul asked dumbfounded.

"Either that or stay pal," the officer raised his voice annoyed.

Saul sighed at the thought of having to leave out to a drug program in shackles. But then he thought about being transferred to a much more civil facility with better necessities and quality of living, which was more reasonable than being locked down in a prison cell twenty-four hours a day.

"Don't worry about the sheets and stuff, the trustee'll take care of it," the officer informed before Saul could think to gather the material.

He cuffed the white inmate through the food slot then ordered him to move forward so he could open the gate. Saul followed instructions and still felt eager to leave despite the manacles he'll be worn on the way out. The gate opened and Saul led the way down the dim hall.

"I won't see ya no more jump-man," Saul shouted to Ali.

Ali decided not to respond, realizing that it would be a waste of breath.

"Thank you very much brotha," Rick said to Ali.

"What?" Ali said, annoyed.

"Not yellin' out like a jackass, knowing the white boy ain't camin' back."

"Oh," Ali replied, settling himself.

"But did you hear that shit?" Rick asked.

"Fuck that white boy," Ali stated harshly.

"I'm not talkin' about y'all little childish argument."

"Oh, 'bout him leavin?" Ali said.

"Never mind Ali," Rick replied, agitated.

"I got all this time in the inside for less shit than what the white boy got?" Jerald exclaimed, confused; "dat's shit ain't fair yo."

"Life ain't fair kid, really doe," remarked Rick.

Chapter 10

Population

After two weeks of lock-up, Jerald's anxiety had subsided a little. He became comfortable and learned how to jail in the little cell. He became familiar with using prison slang and got pumped up from the countless prison stories he had heard.

"Doley," officer Briggs yelled down the wing.

"Yo," Jerald responded.

"Grab your shit; you're goin' to population in a minute."

"Aw'ight," Jerald replied, very unsure if he was up for the challenge of facing the prisoners in population.

"Damn kid, you outta here baby boy," Rick said, "be safe fam, and keep ya ears to the ground and ya head up, that shits mad real in the field out there."

"Handle yours youngin'," Ali encouraged.

"No doubt," J.D replied as he gathered the sheets and blanket off the bunk.

Officer Briggs casually walked down the wing with his hands in his pockets, eyeing some old and some new faced prisoners in their cell as he passed by.

"Let's go Doley, we don't have all day," he ordered impatiently.

"I'm comin'," J.D said nervously.

The officer opened the cell and stepped back so the prisoner could have room to walk out.

"No cuffs?" J. D. asked, curiously.

"If you were going to get fuckin' cuffed I wouldn't be opening the fuckin' cage first...duh!" Briggs remarked sarcastically. "Now head towards the exit gate so you can be told where you're goin'."

"Peace black man," Rick hollered as Jerald was leaving.

"Peace big brah," J. D. yelled back.

"One love son," Ali shouted.

"Yeah, yeah," J. D. replied

When Jerald got to the officer's station outside of the lock-up corridor, he noticed a few riot helmets and sticks placed on a shelf to his right.

"Doley," Blanks called mildly walking up the flight of steps that lead to the first floor unit.

"Yeah," Jerald flinched.

"You know your number?" Blanks asked.

"Nah"

"Well you walk down this flight of steps make the first right and head to center control. They'll tell you where you're going to sleep and whatever else you need to know.

"My number too?" J.D asked.

"Your state number is...let me see here," Blanks said then read from a sheet of paper, "its 11325, got that?" those words rang loud and clear to Jerald.

"Eleven-thirty-two-twenty-five," J.D. repeated, reassuring himself, "you said center is down to my right?"

"Inmate do you know how to fellow instructions or do you need a fuckin' sticker on your chest?" Briggs said rudely.

Jerald gave Officer Briggs an unenthused look, but didn't reply. He threw the pillow case over his shoulder with the linen balled up inside and headed down the steps towards center control, as ordered, without further

113

questions. After being looked up and down by a few passing prisoners, Jerald made it to center control where he approached a big bullet proof window. He stared at several correctional officers who were standing and sitting around, chatting amongst each other. He sensed the tension in the air and was terribly afraid to look around. It felt like he was in a dangerous jungle with nothing but wild hyenas on the prowl for his blood. Nevertheless, he kept his fear to a minimum; he tried not to reflect on all the stories Rick and the other prisoners in lock-up had told him.

" 'Cuse me," he said wearily through a small half oval- shaped opening at the bottom of the big thick glass bubble.

"Yeah, what is it?" A fat, triple-chinned officer responded grumpily as he swirled around in a cushioned, swivel chair. His face resembled Fred Flintstone.

"I, uh, I," Jerald began hesitantly with a dry throat, "I was told to come here; I was in lockup."

"What's your name and number," the fat officer asked sharply.

"Uh, Doley; my number is umm, #11325."

The officer spun back around in the comfortable rolling chair and spoke a few words to the officers. A tall, thin, clean shaved officer, with a gold badge and two stripes on each side of his shirt sleeves, responded to the Fred Flintstone look- alike. The large office turned back around slowly to look at a couple sheets of papers placed

114

on the counter to his left. Jerald stood frozen, not wanting to look around at the few prisoners that walked by. But he was able to see their reflection clearly through the glass.

"Jerald Doley, #11325," the round officer recited for affirmation.

"Yeah," Jerald answered in compliance.

"You'll be going to East Wing, cell #112.

"East Wing, cell #112," Jerald repeated scarcely.

He looked around after that to see four enormous corridors with fifteen-foot steel gates at the front entrance and a mess hall in the center dividing the four units into two sections.

"You know where you're goin?" the officer asked.

"Nah," Jerald replied afraid while praying that he would be escorted to his cell.

"Alright, you see up there at the gate?" the officer pointed his meaty finger to a black sign over top of the fifteen-foot steel gate that had the unit name written in white.

"Yeah," Jerald replied fighting back the butterflies of fear as he while avoided looking at the muscular prisoners that checked him out with icy stares as they walked by.

"You go down the one that says East-wing and see officer Fox; he'll tell you what cell you'll be locking down in," the fat officer explained concisely then turned his attention to the other officers.

Jerald spun back to the glass bubble; he intended to ask the officer another question, but decided that he better not realizing that the officer ignorantly discontinued his communication.

"Shit," Jerald sighed under his breath and moved towards the East-wing corridor.

Chapter 11

East-Wing

Jerald nervously glanced at each prisoner that walked near him. East-wing cell block had three tiers on both sides of the large unit with thirty single cells on each level. Jerald walked timidly down the wing that had five steel tables and four steel seats mounted to each table in the center of the floor. There was a television at each end of the unit. One of the televisions was being watched by a few ghastly looking prisoners who immediately turned their attention to Jerald when he passed to get to the officer's station at the back of the unit. Jerald drew near the six by eight box shaped office with one phone and a walkie-talkie on a small wooden desk and a rolling chair where the officer was seated. On the wall was a red phone for emergency calls in case a fight or a riot broke out.

"'Cuse me," Jerald said politely to the officer seated, reading a *Don Diva* magazine with the door ajar.

"Yeah," the light brown, bald headed, clean shaved officer replied humbly.

"I'm new, umm."

"Okay, you must be uh," the officer looked at his count chart that identified every inmate in his housing unit, "Doley, right?"

"Yeah," Jerald answered.

"What's ya number Doley?"

"Uh, #11325," Jerald answered with a slight feeling of relief from the officer's politeness. He didn't appear to be a jerk-off like some of the other offers he encountered in that facility.

"Alright, Doley, you're in cell #112, that's up these steps on the second level at the beginning of the unit, like three doors from the end, somethin' like that," officer Fox instructed with a slight nod.

"I see you were provided with a state jumper. I'm a see if I can get you some state browns over in a little while. You probably won't see them until after they call out chow."

"Aw'ight," Jerald replied comfortably, and then added, "Do I need a key a somethin' for the door?"

"Nah," Fox smirked and stood at six-feet-two inches, muscular built, "you just go right up, the doors open. You only lock in durin' count and at nine o'clock at night. I'll be bustin' ya door, or anotha officer, so you'll know when you're allowed out, or wanted."

"Do I get a tooth brush and stuff?" Jerald asked to try and drag the questions, praying to be walked to his cell or at least watched until he got in.

"When my runner returns from rec,' he'll get you all that when I send him to get ya browns, alright?"

"Aw'ight," Jerald replied, but still hoped to be rescued or something.

The huge officer went back to reading the magazine. Jerald tossed the linen over his shoulder again. He was wearing a full body jumper like the county jail uniform, but in gray. Blanks had provided him with the jumper before leaving lock-up. Jerald casually, but still nervously, trotted up the near flight of steps to the second level. He walked down the thirty cell length unit in awe of the faces he saw out of his peripheral vision while passing each cell. It was crazy; everything had been depressing at that point, from the gloomy gray color of the walls to the death lurking feeling in his gut.

"Damn," he uttered under his breath and his knees started to weaken like rotting wood. He nearly walked by the cell without realizing it. He opened the heavy, gray painted, steel door that had a thick square-framed window for the officers to see the prisoners through during count. The cell was ten by eleven, with a high

119

ceiling white walls, a steel bunk with a thin mat, a clothing shelf opposite the bunk, a rustic green chest that slid underneath the bunk, a shelf for a television, and, lastly, a thick, barbed-wire window to look outside at the sky and the outer structure of the prison. Jerald glanced around the cell and felt homesickness come over him. He sat down and felt the hard, cold steel bunk through the thin mat. The good thing was he had an extra pillow to avoid cranks in his neck.

"Man, dis shit crazy," he mumbled in dismay.

His thoughts went back for a second to his lavish bedroom he would not see again for eight long years of his life. He jolted quickly from the clanking noise at the steel door. He got up to look out the small framed window and saw the same few prisoners that were watching T.V. looking up at him. A tall, white, blue-eyed, brown haired prisoner had motioned him to come out. Jerald came out the cell timidly and raised his eyebrows, questioning the other prisoner as to what he wanted.

"Yeah," he said.

"Police want you kid," the pale-skinned prisoner told him.

"Oh, ok, thanks," Jerald replied, trying to sound cool and not give the other two prisoners that stared him down with hungry eyes any attention.

"Doley!" Fox called again.

"Yeah"

"I need ya shirt, pants and shoe size. My runner's gonna see if we can getcha stuff before mess," Fox explained, and then gave J.D. a clothing form to fill out.

"You gotta pencil?" Jerald asked.

"Here you go."

"Yo papi," the Spanish accented voice called out from behind.

Jerald spun to the familiar voice.

"Oh, shit, what's up Jose?" Jerald said with a smile of relief.

The fear he held that nearly jumped out his chest had settled a little after seeing someone he knew and could talk too.

"Hey man," Jose shook his head, "you finally made it out dat rat hole."

"Hell yeah, no doubt" Jerald replied happily.

"Bring that paper here when you finish Doley," Fox requested, leaning back into the little padded chair with wheels.

"Aw'ight," Jerald said and walked to the closest table to fill out the paper with Jose.

"I'm the runner in here too papi, this is my house. Deeze is where I was tellin' you about. It's much worst in the other units though. Dis ain't too bad, but you got to watch it. It looks clean and empty, but trust me papi, these guys in here don't' play; you gonna need somethin' in here to protect youself, vultures in here." Jose warned at a low volume as he looked around.

"Like what?" Jerald asked while he wrote slowly and listened carefully.

"Like a banger bro.".

"What's that?" Jerald asked, confused.

"Look bro, what's your name again?"

"J. D."

"Okay, J.D…like a knife is what you need, you can pretty much make it outta anything with an edge on it, you just got to make it sharp, you know," Jose explained quietly, trying not to be heard as he paused between sentences, "but you have to be cool with it bro, understand?"

"Yeah," J.D. replied as his fear started to rise again. Jose saw the anxiety in Jerald's face and wasn't sure if he should be telling him that kind of information; more importantly, he wasn't sure if he should provide Jerald with the material.

"No you don't bro," Jose said sharply; "listen J. D, what I mean is you have to keep your mouth shut… No matter what happens, what you do, you better shut de fuck-up my man. I have peoples that like to take care of rats. Dat's why I'm tellin' you, you have to be cool cuz de pigs like to run down in our cells a lot and tear shit up lookin' for shit dat we not suppose to have. Remember what I'm tellin' you bro, cuz it's important, be cool, but watch ya back, always."

"Aw'ight," J. D. replied comprehensively.

"Okay papi, just chill out. I got you. You finished the form?"

"Yeah," J. D. said as he handed the form over nervously.

"Okay, I'll give it to Fox, so I can get you things from the package room after mess. You go ahead and watch T.V.; I'll get at you later."

"Aw'ight," J. D. said, unsure if he should stay out of his cell or not.

"Oh, and anotha thing bro, don't fuck around with deeze guys at de table down there watchin' T.V, cuz dey trouble. Dey are like de animals I was telling you' about. Si?"

Jerald nodded his head and swallowed hard as he reflected on the insane stories he heard in lock-up. Jose turned around and headed to the officer's station to get Jerald's clothing form signed by officer Fox. J.D. hesitantly walked down to the other end of the unit. Sweat began to trickle down his back, soaking the white State boxer's he was wearing underneath the gray jumper. He wished he hadn't attempted to walk nervously towards the prisoners at the table watching T.V. A five- foot- eleven, slim, light-skinned man with a wavy hair cut crept over to the table Jerald decided to sit at too avoid communication. His name was Sli.

"What's up small time?" Sli grinned sinisterly.

J. D. just gave a head nod without eye contact.

"Yo Moo, we got one cuz'n…fresh bitch in the house," the slim prisoner said jokingly.

The other prisoner smiled, sat like a possum, and was ready to assail his innocent victim. He was a huge black, bald headed, muscular, baby faced convict; he rose slowly from the steel stool showing his massively defined physique, with a tattoo on each thirty-two inch arm, sporting a tight white wife beater, a pair of gray sweat pants and a pair of white socks with slippers.

"What's cookin' crooklin'?" the monster sized prisoner said in a deep voice, smiling from ear to ear and showing one gold tooth in the front with a sixteenth of an inch gap in the center of his grill. J. D. became "Jerald" once he saw how huge the second prisoner stood. He then pretended to play the role of a squirrel and tried to apply the advice Jose had given him.

"Que' pasa, papis?" Jose said with a humorous smile directed at the two troublesome prisoners so they would ease up on their target.

"Juss chillin'," Sli replied a little hyper-actively.

"Just tranna make friends with the little brotha over here," Moose added slowly.

"Okay my friend, dat's my man, be cool. I'll be back Jay," Jose said, then left.

The two troublesome prisoners waited until Jose disappeared off the unit.

"Now back to you little nigga," Sli quickly spoke out with a hostile grin, "cat gotcha tongue a somethin', huh?"

"Look man I don't want no trouble," Jerald exclaimed nervously, still avoiding eye contact.

"Who said we was trouble, small time; you heard my brotha Moose tell the Spanish papi we only tranna make peace," Sli advised dishonestly.

"No, no, nobody," Jerald stuttered as if his thoughts were being read.

"So, so, so we gotta scared one in the house, huh?" Moose smirked with one foot on the steel stool, leaning on his muscled thigh.

"Please man, I don't want no problem. I'm just in here to do my time and go home," Jerald exclaimed fatigued, and nauseous as the knots tightened inside his stomach.

"Problems, problems…ha, ha, ha!" Sli cracked heartily. That's what you had once you got in here lil' nigga, you didn't know! There's nothin' but problems in this hell hole. Every mothafucka in here have problems…and want to go home, but guess what these mothafuckas are home. This is home until the mothafuck'n system fails on them self and not you, nigga. Ha, you fuckin' kid'n me. I'll slap the shit out you, you talk about hav'n no problems again, lil' nigga. And

125

for your info, the system is designed to only fail your black ass."

"Yeah, but we don't have the problem right now," Big Moose included in a provocative way.

"I don't have nothin' man," Jerald said quickly to the vultures.

"Sure you do shorty stock; you just don't know it yet." Moose insisted and poked his huge pointer finger into the table towards Jerald.

"You guys need to back off the kid," the pale skinned prisoner said boldly to the two bullies from a distance and changed the channel on the television.

"You betta back off and mind ya goddamn business boy before I come down on you like a hamma," Moose barked ruthlessly.

"And he definitely won't be alone either pussy," Sli added angrily.

"I'm only a kid man, I'm not lookin' for no hard time, yo," Jerald exclaimed innocently.

"Shut up shorty," Sli tighted his jaw muscles, "you gonna get what you get lil' nigga," he added and pointed his finger at Jerald aggressively.

"You got some shit to say, Mr. Top?" Moose asked the intimidated the white prisoner. Top looked as if he wanted to help but could only sigh deeply and turn his attention back to the television without another word.

"I thought so, before you get yo' ass wiped in here, mothafucka," the gold tooth prisoner said victoriously and stood straight up like a champion.

"Let's go to the private zone," Moose initiated to Slim.

Jerald looked from the huge prisoner to the slim prisoner with fright in his eyes catching the hint between the two.

"Nah, man, I'm not goin' nowhere," Jerald protested as he shook his head disagreeably from side to side.

"Who tellin' to you lil' nigga, huh, shut the fuck-up bitch?" Sli said irritably and moved closer to Jerald, trying to provoke a physical brawl.

"I, I," Jerald began, but noticed Moose when he looked behind him at the officer's station and nodded his head in a go ahead motion to Sli. At that very instant Sli made a swift move and yoked Jerald up from behind in a chicken-wing wrestling hold.

"I don't wanna go nowhere, yo, please stop man, stop yo," Jerald cried out as he tried to break free from Sli's vice-like grip.

"Shut the fuck up lil' nigga before you alert the pigs. Then I'll brake ya fuckin' neck bitch, shut the fuck up pussy," Sli warned Jerald through the grit of his teeth as he tightened the gridlock grip.

"That's not want you want lil' fucker, now let's roll," Moose warned angrily.

127

"Please, man, please, I don't have nothing," Jerald begged in a muffled tone.

Sli held a grip on Jerald that nearly caused him to pass out. He immediately straightened his arms out like bird wings.

"No, no, no!" Jerald tried to scream out vehemently, hoping that officer Fox would hear him, but, to no avail, his words weren't audible enough to be heard. Jose strolled back on the unit a couple seconds too late with a brown paper bag in his hand.

"What was that noise, yo?" he asked the frizzy, brown haired Caucasian prisoner. Top shrugged and shook his head without words. Jose picked up the prisoner's body language quickly and didn't see the other three in sight.

"Fuck, I told him to keep his eyes open, fuck man," Jose exclaimed angrily and rubbed his hands through his jet black hair.

"They bullied him dude, grabbed him right up, it was nothing he could do," Top managed to say scarcely.

"Fuck, Top, why you didn't help him, bro?"

"Come on Ace, you know the deal; it, it, it'll be war in here dude. These fuckin' guys, they're, they're ass holes. I did say somethin' but they, you know. I, I just backed off man."

"I got you bro, fuck it, fuck it; I'll be right back," Jose said and walked off the unit in a hurry.

Ten minutes had past; Top fiddled with his fingers quietly as he sat on top of a steel table, staring blankly at the television screen. Moose walked out from the dark smiling to himself like he was very pleased with life. He went to sit at one of the steel tables, but stopped mid-way.

"What the fuck you lookin' at white boy, you want some of this?" he barked at Top for eyeing him disgustedly.

Top sighed hard, curled his lips to the side, and turned back to the television to avoid what could be a serious situation.

"Yeah, exactly," Moose exclaimed.

The other bully came out the dark corner and looked around to make sure that officer Fox wasn't walking up and down the unit.

"Word up, fam!" Sli said loudly for Top to hear, "nobody betta botha her, I mean him."

"Sho nuff, they bet not," Moose added, as a matter of fact.

Jerald walked out the corner weakly a few minutes later holding his stomach, with a black eye, tears streaming down his cheeks and a bloody noise. Jose returned at the same time to see Jerald in a horrible condition. He walked over to Jerald quickly.

"Yo bro, here take this bag, you got soap, a wash cloth, towel, and clothes. I, I don't even want to ask what happened...it's you...man, fucking jokers man. I told you bro!" Jose stammered furiously, hoping that it wasn't what he anticipated it to be by looking at Jerald's appearance.

"What is it to you, Ace?" Sli asked and turned his eyebrows up.

"You talkin' to me, maricon?" Jose said, and took a couple steps towards Sli returning the malevolent look.

"No other," Sli said provokingly, not a worried look on his face.

"Yeah, whatever bruh, you don't see no woman here, I can tell you dat now." Jose pointed his finger aggressively.

"I see what I wanna see, when I wanna see it, and how I wanna see it," Sli replied harshly.

"Not while I'm in here bro, fuck dat shit, carbon," Jose said tensely, drawn out of his humble character.

"And whose gonna stop him, papi?" the beastly bully stood up to intervene and crossed his arms masterfully.

Without anymore words from either prisoner, nearly fifteen cell doors opened at once on both sides of the unit on each tier with nothing but Latinos. They stepped out silently and stared at both bullies without moving an inch more, waiting for Jose to give them the word.

"What you mean my man?" Jose said calmly, like a godfather in control. "Like I said bro, you don't see no woman while I'm in here, dis shit ain't San Quinton, you not going to take what's not given voluntarily. All dat other shit, I don't understand. I told you before dis is my lil homie, dat should have been e'nuff to let you know to back off."

"Shhhhit," Sli uttered as he looked around at all the Spanish prisoners that stood like troopers in front of their cell doors, "let's go back to the cut Moo," he added in a retreat mode.

"Yeah, we'll see you later shorty stock" Moose said emotionless to Jerald, but looked at Jose as though he won that battle, but not the war.

A short, thick, bald headed Spanish prisoner said a few words to Jose, with hand gestures that only the Spanish clique were able to understand. Jose responded with the same hand movement, and the entire Spanish clique stepped back in their cell simultaneously.

"Shit man," Jerald cried and tightened his fist with the hand that wasn't clinched around his stomach. He was distraught by the event he had never experienced before in his life. He kept rewinding the event in his mind: "I'm a guy, I'm a fuckin' guy". But the fact remained that two bullies, who spent more than half their lives in and out of prison, didn't care.

"I told you to stay alert, bro. These fuckin' guys are animals," Jose spat with frustration.

Jerald explained painfully, "They grabbed me in a choke hold, and…and," he sobbed as he tried to get the rest out.

"Shit, it'll be okay bro; I got somethin' for you in case dey try to kick dat shit off again if I'm not around." Jose said quietly.

Top got up and walked to the sixth cell from the entrance on the first level. Jose paused, looked around, and only noticed the eyes of his Latino brothers staring through the steel door of their cell. He showed Jerald a long piece of metal wrapped tightly, with black electric tape around the handle.

"I can't use that," Jerald said nervously.

"Look bro, it's cither this or go through what just happened again, your choice. I wouldn't think nothin' about it dis time if it happens." Jose paused, "Let me tell you bro, I seen a young guy like you get gutted behind bullshit like dis. Your choice; live or let live"

He stopped again and quickly handed Jerald the long dagger.

"Keep dis in the front of you boxer's inside your jumper. When you lock in, you can probably hide it under you toilet or get some tape from somewhere and tape it under you bunk. You catch what dey call a astro charge for dis piece of metal," Jose explained clearly then added, "it's up to you bro, dis is some ad-seg time if you get caught, so use it or lose it, ok papi?."

"Yeah," Jerald mumbled, unsure about the entire situation and used the sleeve of his jumper to wipe the blood from his noise.

"Are you okay, bro?" Jose asked

132

"Yeah, my eye hurts a little. Dat skinny mothafucka sucka punched me in the eye man."

"Dey have to pay one way or de other papi, you got to watch you self closer for now on."

"I know," Jerald said through clinched teeth.

The struggle flashed back to his memory. His chest began to burn inside like fire; he was violated of his manhood. The vain in his temple pulsated from anger, but what could he do? What had been done was over; however, he swore underneath his breath from deep down that nothing like that would happen to him again, no matter what. How could he have run into something so inhumane that soon? It was like a tale for the HBO series *Oz*. He heard a lot about Trenton State Prison while on the streets but he never anticipated himself walking through the gates of one violent institution. If anything, he felt he should have been serving his time in a less maximum security facility, like Bordentown or Yardville.

"Now, go to your cell and clean up before Fox comes out and questions you. Deeze pigs will put you in the hole for lookin' like you do; dey know dat somethin' happened to you dat wasn't supposed to, whether you told 'em or not," Jose suggestively warned.

Jerald took the banger from Jose and walked up to his cell, unsure if the two bullies where watching him from the dark. Top came back out his cell and glad to not have gotten into something that wasn't his business.

"Will the kid be alright, Ace?"

Jose rolled his eyes and didn't respond; he felt Jerald's situation wasn't worth discussing with a cowardly prisoner that didn't get down for a good cause.

"Bueno amigo," Jose said to the short stocky Latino prisoner, who stepped back out of his cell after Top.

"No problemo, bro. the next time dey start bullshit, we comin' down strong, no rap," the Latino leader replied back seriously, then returned inside his cell. Jose quickly looked at Top.

"Keep an eye on de young boy til I get back, but he should be okay."

"You sure the kid'll be alright Ace?" Top asked.

"It's do or get done...again, he will be ok," Jose replied seriously, then left in a hurry.

"Shit, you got that right," Top huffed under his breath with the look of a twenty year veteran drug user.

Moose and Sli nonchalantly walked back out from their cubby-hole. Both prisoners were stoned on heroin; it felt good to escape the reality of their imprisonment.

"I'm feelin' good as hell now, Moo," Sli grinned and scratched at his face and neck slowly.

"Not me," Moose objected, lazy-eyed. "Ace, got to pay for interferin' in our biz."

"No doubt, and so does this bitch ass mothafucka here," Sli nodded at Top; "they can't tell us what to do, fuck that shit, young'n is mine," he added boldly.

"Ours nigga," Moose corrected harshly.

"Yeah, right...ours," Sli rectified quickly and glanced around the unit dumbfounded, "now where is shorty stock anyway."

"Top!" Moose called aggressively.

"What?" Top answered, annoyed, as he turned around to face the bully down.

Moose chuckled heartily for a second at the so-called threatening stare the white prisoner had given him.

"Where's shorty stock?" Moose demanded as he swelled his chest up.

"I'm not my brothers' keeper,' Top responded back sarcastically.

"We didn't ask you all that, did we?" Sli said, positioning to rack the white prisoner up.

"Whatever," Top sighed.

Jerald stepped out of his cell bravely this time aware of the two bullies' wicked stare burning through his jumper.

"Well, well, well," Sli began enthused to see the youngster didn't hide out all night, "look what the prison has warehoused, Moo."

135

"Yeah, I'm seein'!" Moose laughed and allowed the substance to take its effect. Jerald took the long way down the tier towards the officer's station. He walked a little slowly with a limp and rolled up the sleeves to his jumper past his elbows. Sli stood at attention and watched Jerald with of laughter in his heart.

"Oh, oh, she's hard now," he said with a smirk; "well, we gonna see about this shit."

"Wait up for me, I gotta drop some mud," Moose said. "I'll be right back, chill out." The heroin always affected Moose's stomach and caused him to go to the bathroom.

"Listen Moo, go do what you gotta do, cuz I'm gonna do me," Sli said in a slick manner and stuck his tongue out like a snake.

"Hold up nigga, damn," Moose exhaled hard; "I gotta take a shit. Fuck, dig, you suppose to wait for me, ain't no if, ands, whats about it," he added in a deep tone.

"I will, I will, cool out fam. I'm a just prepare the little mothafucka for us, that's all…ha, ha, ha," Sli boasted.

"Yea, you do that!" Moose agreed, big-eyed, "I won't be long, now don't bull shit me. I gotta go shit before you'll be helpin' me clean it up right here."

Sli laughed and clapped his hands playfully, as if it was a good joke. "I will have this lil' nigga over in the cut when you get back."

"Be there too. I'll be back," Moose pointed to Sli's forehead and headed to the back of the tier on the third floor. He quickly trotted up the three flights of stairs, anxious to get back down. Jerald slowly watched from where he sat, still not taking his eyes off of the thin, cocky prisoner. Top felt the tension rise as Jerald stared coldly at his adversary. Top shook his head because he knew Sli had something up his sleeve for the young prisoner.

"Yo, kid," Top said to Jerald, "Ace told me to tell ya he'll be right back."

Jerald nodded his head in response; he felt the eerie tension coming from the sneaky prisoner. Top nodded back as he realized what was going down. It didn't call for his service, so he walked away and minded his own business without saying a word.

"Step the fuck off nigga," Jerald said strongly, through gritted teeth.

"Ooooh, Oookay," Sli said with laughter and moved closer to the table Jerald was sitting. "So we tough now, huh? Let's go small stock, before I fuck you up right here."

"I just told you to back the fuck up," Jerald repeated slowly with conviction and looked down at the table, but kept Sli in his peripheral.

Sli, unbelievably, tried the same tactical move on Jerald without his partner being there.

"Nooooo," Jerald yelled angrily at the top of his lungs. It seemed as if Jerald was in a scene from a movie where everything was in slow motion. Jerald whipped out the sharp piece of taped metal from his jumper and repeatedly stabbed Sli in the abdominal area with rage. Sli screamed in pain, but more so in shock; his life flashed before him like an uncontrolled movie projector.

"Ahhhhhh," Sli coughed, as blood sprayed through his fingers on both hands from his stomach. His eyes opened wide, and then closed; his jaws locked and blood oozed out of the corner of his mouth.

Sli fell to his knees, stunned that his life ended by the hands of a young prisoner, a kid at that. He could only say slowly, "You little mothafucka. How could you."

"No more, you bitch as nigga! Die mothafucka, die! You fuckin'pussy!" Jerald shouted violently and backed away from the falling prisoner.

Officer Fox heard the shout, jumped up immediately, and looked out on the unit. Then he quickly picked up the red phone and instantly sounded the institution alarm. Immediately, he spoke into the phone and called the prison code for the other correction officers to respond at once.

Moose exited his cell quickly to see what had caused the alarm to sound. He had a bad feeling, something he never felt before since he's had been in prison. He bolted down stairs to see his partner lying face down on the cold concrete in a pool of blood. Moose's eyes flared; his mind searched for reasons of how his friend found death so sudden when he had just talked to him five minutes before. He knew that there was always a possibility of death in prison, but he never imagined himself, or his right-hand man, ending it like that. He ignored the alarm, which prisoners in every correctional institution are forbidden to do. He disregarded Officer Fox's barely audible order over the screaming alarm to get back to his cell.

"Oh shit, Sli, what the fuck!" Moose cried, unable to rationalize the scene.

He ran over to the bloody body that twitched a few times before its last evidence of life left. The steel doors to the prison cells locked before Fox ran down the unit; therefore, every prisoner that had been relaxing in his cell could only look out the small window to see what had taken place. Fox ran in a hurry; he stayed cautious of the violent prisoners that didn't pay attention to his order. Fox opened a secluded unit gate, which was unauthorized for inmates, so the riot guards could enter.

"Get down! Get down now, right now!" Fox shouted at J.D. and Moose, who listened with deaf ears.

Suddenly a team of correctional officers ran on the unit in full force, dressed in riot gear, holding thick black beat-down sticks tightly in hand. Jerald stood and watched Sli gargle his last breath, oblivious to everything that took place around him. He was still holding the evidence in hand, unaware of the bloody responsibility that lied before him. A three hundred pound officer yanked Moose up from the back with a stick under his throat and took him down to the floor, hard, unconcerned if he was innocent or not. Briggs and Blanks ran in after the riot gang.

"Holy macro," Briggs shouted, surprised that Jerald was involved.

Fox grabbed Jerald up at the same time Moose was being wrestled to the concrete. He cuffed Jerald, with the help of a few officers, and dragged him to the gray painted concrete after taking the murder weapon away. Briggs kneeled by the stiff body to check its pulse.

"Call the medics!" he yelled.

Three commanding officers stepped through the crowd: a brown haired, blue- eyed, baby- face Sergeant, with two stripes on each sleeve and a gold badge on his shirt; a gray haired, gray mustached, six-foot officer, with a single gold bar on each shoulder, who was second in command followed; and a five-foot eleven, baby-face, cigar smoking, spectacle-wearing, three hundred pound Captain, with gold badges and stars all over his shirt, with a facial expression that said a lot about his demeanor towards prisoners.

"Lock the entire goddamn prison down," the captain yelled after he viewed the dead body.

Fox began to explain what he witnessed and showed the murder weapon at the same time to the ranked officers.

"It's not my fault!" Jerald shouted as anger swelled in his eyes, his face buried in the concrete by two officers.

"Tell it to the fuckin' judge, pal," Briggs shouted back at him while the other officers stared at Jerald and whispered amongst each other.

Moose lied quietly, transfixed at the corpse of his friend in a pool of blood. He will never be as close to another prisoner ever again like he was with Sli. It was over, he thought; the side kick he never had growing up until this last prison bid was dead. All the prisoners, including Jose, who was ordered to lock-in during the riot team entrance, began tapping their cups on the cell doors once the alarm stopped. That meant life was over for a long term prisoner.

Jerald didn't understand that his life was on the line from that point on inside the prison system. He was definitely unaware of the association Moose and Sli had with the other prisoners, who would retaliate blood for blood. Jerald felt a great deal of fear; he felt anger, he felt violated, and all the above. It really didn't matter anymore; he was doing time in the inside, so this is how it had to go down. He cried deeply inside as he reflected on how things happened so fast: sleeping in a queen size bed, to driving a brand new car, to having money and different girls, and now to murdering predators in a state penitentiary to protect his own life.

Chapter 12

Ad-Seg

Three months had gone by since Jerald sat in solitary confinement before seeing court line (court is where one civilian officer who is assigned as an institution judge sentences every prisoner that is charged with an institutional sanction for violation of rules). Confinement seemed like a lifetime to Jerald: eating three kid size meals a day, taking two showers a week, and having no privileges. He couldn't wait to see the court line officer because in his mind he knew that what he did was right. There was no way he would get in serious trouble for protecting himself. All he had to do was explain what caused him to kill the other prisoner; they would let him back in population and he would gain a powerful reputation to not be fucked with from then on. "This shit is mad real," he thought after the court line hearing.

"That mothafucka crazy," he laughed out of anger; it was not yet clear to him what had just happened. Defending himself against someone who violated his manhood was too raw to handle.

The day went by in that little eight-by-ten cell without a window, the stench smell of urine mixed with funk, and no one to socialize with. Jerald finally came to grips with how court line had served him earlier that morning. He refused to eat all three meals thinking about who, when, what, and why, and how he's going to tell his mother. How was he going tell her he had to do life in prison without the possibility of parole for first degree murder? How was he going to explain to her still having to serve ten years of his time in Administration Segregation (Ad-Seg), with limited visitations, before re-entering another prison population? He didn't know how he was going to do it. The walls felt like they were going to close in on him. A thick smell of dirty, urine, funk, and bad food was clogging his wind pipes. He stayed sane through the realization of it all because he still had a mother who needed to see him, and a baby sister and older sister who would come visit him soon enough.

"Get ya butt up and do somethin' with ya self and stop drivin' that damn car around with no license!" he vividly remembered his mother saying, as he curled up on the bunk with tears streaming down his cheeks. "Why

143

couldn't I be home hearing those words again", he cried inside, feeling emotionally distraught.

THE END OF A LONG BEGINNING....

PART 1

"Circumstances don't make a person; it only brings out what was always in them"

Anonymous….. A.C

"A Person is never who they say they are; they're who they show them self to be"

Anonymous…..Boro

"There's always room for change"

L.E.F….

www.ingramcontent.com/pod-product-compliance
Lightning Source LLC
Chambersburg PA
CBHW020643250626
47154CB00008B/2786